SMOKEY KINGFISH
and the Sinking Island

A NOVEL BY JON CARDEN

SMOKEY KINGFISH and the SINKING ISLAND

© 2005 smokeykingfish.com

Published by:

smokeykingfish.com
7 Le Clos des Chenolles
Les Chenolles
St John
Jersey, Channel Islands
BRITISH ISLES
JE3 4FB

All rights reserved. No part of this publication may be reproduced or transmitted in any form or by any means or stored in any retrieval system of any nature without prior written permission obtained from the publisher. Application for permission for other use of copyright material, including permission to reproduce extracts in other published works shall be made to the publisher. Full acknowledgement of author, publisher and source must be given.

This book was completed July 2004. Whilst much of the content was inspired by historical events, those events occurred in the late nineteenth and early twentieth century. Any similarity to events occurring or to people living since this time is purely coincidental.

British Library Cataloguing-in-Publication Data
A catalogue record for this book is available from the British Library

ISBN 0955114705

Photos by Jon Carden

Printed and bound in the UK by Tandem Press
www.tandempress.com

'Whispering wind ... metallic sea

Storm's Herald driving me

Others sought ... others found

Spins us all ... round and round

Towards the land to rise and strain

As Watersplash

Once again'

PROLOGUE

Watersplash was dead.

But what of his life?

Days earlier it had begun. Out at sea ... out beyond a dark continent in the vastness of a Great Ocean.

There, for a short time, all had been calm. Inevitably though, a wind had grown ... and as it grew ... from whisper to roar... so Watersplash was created.

And once begun ... for six days the wind never let up. It made Watersplash strong and drove him East along ancient tracks.

And during that time, Watersplash encountered no land ... neither atoll nor isle to stifle his progress or deflect him away from his true path.

But that soon changed.

Inevitably, Watersplash reached the Morningtarian Continental Shelf.

But he was not for turning back.

Instead, Watersplash charged across it ... confounding the outer reefs stood sentry to grey massed ranks of sea cliff and storm beach, and finally - heroically - reared up strong and proud against those insurmountable obstacles ... and was smashed.

Watersplash died ... but Watersplash's wake was still to come. Experience gleaned from his great journey imprinted onto the next wave ... and the next.

Slowly but not quite infinitely, Watersplash's predecessors chipped away at the foundation from which Morningtaria rose and the fragments of that Dark Continent shattered and flaked away.

CHAPTER ONE

'What's for dinner Mum?'

'Sausage and Beans, Smokey ... your favourite!'

'YIPPPEEEE!!'

Smokey Kingfish was stoked.

'Oooh ... MAGIC!' he hooted.

Smokey loved Sausage and Beans.

'And Chips?'

'Drat!' Bernice cursed under her breath before turning away from the two ring stove to the fridge from which she extracted a bag of "Herbert Biggs' Jumbo Chips".

'Of course Smokey.'

'YAHOOOO!!'

... because if there was one thing Smokey loved more than Sausage and Beans ... it was Sausage, Beans and Chips!

Bernice, hurriedly prepared the Chips. It was extra work but she didn't feel put out.

'It'll be ready in ten minutes Pumpkin!'

'Nice one mum!'

Bernice smiled. A kind word from Smokey, her only son ... a son she doted on ... was enough to make her sing.

'Sausage and beans,
Chips and ketchup too.
A lovely meal for one
Much better for two!'

The doorbell rang.

'Can you get that for me Pumpkin?'

'Ok Mum.'

Smokey got up and took the four paces from the sofa to the front door.

It was George the Postman.

'A parcel for Smokey Kingfish.'

'That's me!'

'Sign here soldier!'

Smokey took George's pen and printed his name in letters altogether too large for the signature box at the bottom of the Delivery Docket.

'SMOKEY KINGFISH'

'Nice one boss!'

And with a skip and a smile the happy Posty went on his way.

'Has it arrived, Smokey?'

He held the package at arms length.

It seemed to Smokey as if he had been waiting his whole life for this package.

'Yes mum.'

****

Smokey, along with his mum, his dad and five million other souls were Muddleheads and they lived in Morningtaria.

On the whole, the Muddleheads of Morningtaria were simple folk.

They lived in flats and houses, went to work, enjoyed sport and loved to watch the telly.

As a rule the Muddleheads were a rather dull and stupid bunch. That much was obvious to an outsider, but not to the Muddleheads themselves. No ... they thought they were clever ... because of the gadgets they made ... even cultured because the municipal buildings they never bothered to visit, housed a lot of musty old books and relics.

Most stupid of all, The Muddleheads thought themselves to be spiritual ... because they dreamed of an after-life filled with Beer and Chocolate.

To sum up, the Muddleheads of Morningtaria were simple-minded and shallow and this lead to turbulence and upheaval.

... Just as shallowness at sea does likewise.

****

Just what had arrived in the post that lunchtime?

The date was a giveaway. It was Smokey's seventeenth birthday.

It was Affiliation Day ... the day Smokey became a Club Member.

But which Club was he to become a member of?

That was the question Smokey asked himself as he stood in the hallway trembling with nervous anticipation and holding a brown paper package in his outstretched hands that beckoned to be opened.

'Which Club?'

Bernice emerged from the kitchen. She placed loving hands on her son's shoulders, nuzzled her face against his and stared down at the parcel.

'Let it be something special' she pleaded inwardly.

But deep down she knew it would not be.

The Kingfish's were not special and you had to be special to become a member of a special club.

For the most part, the clubs of Morningtaria were nothing more than ordinary groups of ordinary people doing ordinary things. Indeed, the majority of clubs were so very ordinary; they were nothing more than a group of Muddleheads in the same job.

But not all.

There were exceptions and the biggest exception of all was the Bosspig's Club.

Bernice had dreamt her son might one day become a Bosspig.

They WERE special.

Even the clothes the Bosspigs wore singled them out as a cut above.

'Yes indeed!' fantasised Bernice 'Incandescent Indigo Trousalschmoks and Elongated Orificial Overpipes.' She pictured Smokey in those fantastic garments.

'Very smart ... very smart indeed!'

But Bernice was not to know that clothes do not maketh the man, for despite the spectacular appearance of your average Bosspig, theirs was a club shrouded in mystery, shadow and abject weirdness.

She would never have guessed that beyond the public's gaze, the Bosspigs performed secret rituals, formed seedy societies and greeted each other with funny handshakes ... and whilst it was true the leisure loving Bosspigs, as so vividly portrayed in the glossy magazines Bernice devoured, spent an inordinate amount of time enjoying themselves at glitzy parties, in top restaurants, or at the racetrack ... they were equally happy pleasuring themselves in slightly 'weirder' pursuits ... the most popular requiring the secret acquisition of garments tailor-made from the finest leather and endowed with studs and large button holes which were stitched into places where studs and large button holes had no right being stitched.

Those Bosspigs attended secret liaisons in discrete locations to which they brought those garments ... as well as cheese and short lengths of hose-piping the width of small furry rodents.

What they got up to in those meetings was anyone's guess but even the most unobservant of Muddleheads, Bernice included, could not fail to notice that many a Bosspig they happened across, walked with rather a wide gait, as if they were balancing invisible balloons between their knees.

What Bernice also failed to understand was that when the Bosspigs weren't busying themselves being weird, they were busying themselves in every other Muddlehead's business.

In short, they ran the show.

By fair means or foul, they controlled everything.

The Bosspigs even decided which club a Muddlehead joined.

Indeed, it was they who had sent Smokey his package ... a package which contained a Club Membership Card.

An identity card.

More than that ... Smokey's new identity.

By determining which club Smokey was to join, the card would soon dictate what he should look like, who he should see, what he should do and what he should think ... for the rest of his life!

The Bosspigs had a motto, 'Divide ... and rule'.

They were in charge.

****

Smokey Kingfish tore open the package.

He pulled out a small plastic card and read the indented words on its face:-

| **SMOKEY KINGFISH** |
| **SURFER** |

He flipped it over.

On the reverse, Smokey saw his own holographic image.

The picture showed a skinny youth whose body contours betrayed an indifference to physical exercise and affinity for the sweet snacks and fatty meals so cherished by the children of Morningtaria.

Smokey had a soft baby face, startlingly bright blue eyes and blonde hair which the holograph extended into greasy, shoulder-length curtains.

In contrast to Smokey's hairless face, the image sowed upon his chin a bushy Billy goat beard. Finally, it dressed him in a black wetsuit and placed a surfboard under his arm.

The hologram transformed Smokey.

No longer the innocent child – an orphan child at that – who had lived with foster parents from the age of six months. Smokey was reinvented by the holograph into a beer-swilling, wave-hogging, bushpig 'stoinking' Morningtarian Wave Warrior.

It was so exciting!

Smokey had waited all his life to be somebody and now he was!

****

As well as his identity, Smokey Kingfish's package contained a letter instructing him to go that very afternoon to Turd Cove – the Morningtarian Surf Beach – for orientation and enrolment into Surf School.

Smokey's eyes lit up.

'So soon? YIPPEEE!' ... and with that, he kissed his mum on the cheek, ran straight out the front door, down Bobo Street to the bus station, where he took a number 14B, alighting at the Turdtown Harbour from where he walked the short distance to Turd Cove.

****

Some minutes later as she sat in front of the telly with a double portion of Sausage, Beans and Chips bulging from the plate on her lap, Bernice began to cry.

CHAPTER TWO

Surf School didn't take long. In fact Smokey along with the rest of his class graduated with honours around teatime the same day.

By then ... apparently... they had learned all there was to learn about surfing.

Which wasn't very much at all.

In Morningtaria, whilst the surfers concerned themselves with the catching and riding of waves ... any similarity to the skilful and historic pursuit of wave-riding for its own sake ... ended right there.

The Muddleheads knew of surfing only as the simplest of team sports - practised exclusively at the Morningtarian dedicated surf beach, Turd Cove - a two hundred metre crescent of oily sand, poo-stained ocean and putrefying humanity.

In The Cove, only six surfers - two teams of three - were permitted to enter the water at any one time.

And that was only on Match Days.

Twice a week ... sometimes once if a Match Day clashed with a Bosspig Public Holiday, the full compliment of Morningtaria's surfers assembled.

There on the beach, they watched - patiently waiting their turn - as successive teams entered the water, took part in their match, then left the water.

Each and every match commenced when the players paddled out ... not just anywhere mind you ... but corralled into a field of play barely ten metres wide extending from shore to a line positioned beyond the breaking waves.

As the surf along the remainder of Turd Cove went unridden, the surfers clustered together, like Seals tangled in a discarded fishing net, panicking as they waited for the match to begin.

When a suitable wave rolled into the field of play, the match referee - who was seated in a concrete tower on the beach - identified it as the 'Match Wave' by pressing a button on his control panel which illuminated the wave via two dozen spotlights attached to the seabed.

At this point, the surfers turned towards the beach and frantically started to paddle.

More often than not, the wave chosen by the referee, even on the most perfect of surfing days, was a pitiful close-out.

Not that it really mattered.

The wave was largely irrelevant.

Assuming the surfers even caught it, they did not ride it as a surfer was meant to ride a wave. It was never ridden for what it was. A surfer didn't extol years of knowledge or experience in the judgement of how it might break.

No.

Once up and riding, they didn't even bother to look at it!

The 'Match Wave' was reduced to a mere jousting horse … a vehicle for two teams to ride whilst beating the living daylights out of one another.

It was easy to conclude the Match had little to do with surfing.

All that mattered was winning and this was achieved by the team whose Runner made it first to shore, with the assistance of his Blocker, having survived the onslaught of the opposing team's Tackler.

Smokey learnt and understood these things easily.

What he also learnt but did not fully comprehend was the concept of 'Sole Surfing'.

His teacher at surf school had touched briefly on the subject.

'Sole Surfing' he had said 'Is the act of riding a wave by oneself - a very silly thing to do!'

Further, upon a cursory glance of the 'Surfer's Rule Book', Smokey had discovered that 'Sole Surfing' was, in fact, illegal. Indeed, it was even mentioned in the Morningtarian Penile Code as a 'Public Order Offence' and the statutory penalty for all 'P.O.O's' was to have one's head exploded!

When he thought about it, Smokey couldn't imagine why anyone would want to breach the rules of the brilliant 'game' of surfing ... let alone bother to do it on their lonesome.

To do so would be weird.

But what of the consequence?

A bit harsh maybe?

Well, Smokey didn't much worry about that. On the contrary, he found himself happily speculating about his own head blowing up and what a terrific gag that might prove to be.

'All my mates would have a right laugh' he daydreamed 'I'd be the toast of Turd Cove!'

'Besides' Smokey chuckled to himself 'those buffoons from the Municipal Surf Lifesavers Club would have to clean up the mess afterwards ... WHAT A HOOT!'

CHAPTER THREE

Smokey again considered 'Sole Surfing' as he sat one sunny afternoon on the warm sands of Turd Cove.

By now, he had been a surfer for three months, knew all there was to know about surfing and was, in his own mind at least, the best runner in the Minor Surf League.

Smokey also knew his place on the surfer's pecking order and didn't much like it, wedged as he was between the fat smelly blocker from his own team and a pimply faced lady boy who rode a bodyboard, was not in a team and was only allowed onto the beach because, it was rumoured, one of the referees enjoyed fumbling inside the lad's underpants.

Smokey hated his lowly position. He was desperate to move up the ranks ... to become a legend, just like his hero, Sammy Bagpipes, who had been a champion runner until George Pickle, an overzealous Turd Cove 'Lifeguard' had mistaken Bagpipes for a shark and thrown a hand grenade at him ... despite the fact that Bagpipes had been sitting on the beach at the time ... eating Poptarts.

Smokey wanted to be like Bagpipes ... wanted his name repeated in hushed admiration just like Bagpipes'.

'Gee!' they had said 'did you see Bagpipes' last match? Did you see how he zigzagged to the shore? What a legend, hey?'

It made Smokey all gooey just thinking about it and so he decided something had to be done ... something unique and daring which might make him a 'legend' too.

Thoughts of personal safety and self preservation never entered Smokey's mind ... but that was only to be expected because Smokey, a Muddlehead, didn't really have one.

Well ... that's not quite true.

He had a mind ... but not the enquiring, thought-filled thingy one might define as such.

No. Smokey's mind contained no independent or free-flowing thought, but thoughts linked like hermaphrodite worms in a shag ring ... by the pricks of ignorance, propaganda and prejudice.

To put it another way, Smokey did not worry about such things as head explosions. To think otherwise, he had long ago concluded, was cowardly.

Not surprising really. His was a gung-ho attitude shared by the majority of Muddleheads ... and encouraged in no small measure by the Bosspigs.

Indeed, The Bosspigs undertook successive propaganda campaigns in order to promote the virtues of courage, nationalism and machismo.

It was all for a purpose ... so that in time of war, Smokey and his peers might enthusiastically sign up for soldiering ... which, of course, suited the Bosspigs just fine. They regarded war as a jolly and lucrative jape and blustered their way into as many as possible ... preferably against the smaller and weaker island nations to the North of Morningtaria.

What better for The Bosspigs, in their desire to exterminate the odd fuzzy nation, than to encourage a steady supply of patriotic boofheads to do the deed on their behalf?

Smokey Kingfish most definitely fell into the category of 'Boofhead'... as amply demonstrated when, for no better reason than to impress his friends, he came up with an idea ... a most stupid idea.

By the time Smokey left the beach that sunny afternoon, he had a plan ...

A plan which he executed the very next morning.

****

As the new sun rose expectantly over the tenement rows, Smokey shut his front door, strolled purposefully down Bobo Street, caught the 14B for the hundredth time to the Turdtown Harbour, from where he walked the short walk to Turd Cove, paddled out into the surf, took off and rode a beautiful eight foot high left peeling wave to the beach ... alone.

> 'Slowly, but not quite infinitely, Watersplash's predecessors chipped away at the foundation from which Morningtaria rose and the fragments of that dark Continent shattered and flaked away.'

When that morning Smokey Kingfish rode a wave alone, the wave was Watersplash and the fragment doing the flaking off was Smokey.

****

A few minutes later, as he stood at the water's edge, the foam from spent waves dancing over his toes, expectation as to what he might feel the instant his head was relieved of its contents was replaced by surprise when instead, Smokey was arrested, ushered from the beach by a Bosspig's Enforcement Officer, bundled into a large black motor car, driven to Turdtown Harbour and escorted onto a cargo ship where he was locked inside a cabin for three days until the vessel weighed anchor and set sail.

****

Something was not quite right and Smokey knew it.

His head was still on his shoulders.

'How could this be?' he wondered as he sat within the confines of his small but perfectly comfortable cabin.

Smokey had witnessed a number of head explosions during his lifetime but never had he considered they were triggered by somebody, let alone that that somebody was an ever-present, all-seeing authority.

No, to Smokey, head explosions were simply the result of doing that which you were not supposed to ... just as a stomach full of Sparky Bars resulted in a face full of pimples ... rule breaking and head explosions were a simple case of 'cause and effect'.

Smokey also harboured a vague suspicion that the Enforcement Officer who had arrested him was not quite as he first appeared.

After all, the Enforcers were members of an elite Club who revelled in their own authority and, who it seemed, enjoyed nothing better than to meter out their own sadistic justice onto all and sundry. From bloodying the noses of over-enthusiastic Bongoball fans ... to assassinating graffiti artists and skateboarders, the Enforcers could always be relied on to do their duty.

But not this one.

On the contrary, Smokey's assailant had not mistreated him, had ensured that whilst locked in his cabin, he received three good meals a day and through a gentle demeanour had conveyed to Smokey a feeling that everything would turn out just fine.

To Smokey, it was all very strange.

CHAPTER FOUR

Ninety six hours after setting sail, a small island emerged on the horizon to the North.

Smokey, who had been allowed to roam freely around the Cargo Ship since leaving port, was informed by Skipper Kipper, the captain, that the island ahead of them was called Penisle 102 and it was to be his new home.

Smokey's head dropped as he cast a despondent eye over Penisle 102.

As they drew closer, he saw an island encircled by a white sand beach and backed by a seemingly impenetrable wall of jungle. Smokey saw no sign of civilisation on that land and unhappily concluded that his fate was to be that of sad and lonely castaway, marooned for life on what amounted to little more than a large rock.

Skipper Kipper, somewhat lifted Smokey's spirits when, with a rather uncomfortable monologue pertaining to Muddlehead philanthropy, he explained that the huge container secured on the ship's deck was a survival pack containing provisions to sustain Smokey on the island indefinitely.

Kipper, reading from the SS Bulldog's shipping manifest outlined those provisions ...

Inflatable house (1)
First-aid kit (1)
Bamburgers (10,000)
Minnie Fergy Pizzas (10,000)
Sparky Bars (10,000)

He continued ...

'In accordance with charitable Muddlehead credo, you have also been provided with such items necessary for the maintenance of your identity ...'

Surfboards (30)
Tropical surfboard wax (1,000)
Clothing packages (100)

Smokey's ears pricked up when he heard about the clothing packages.

They were, according to Kipper, to be opened half-yearly and contained surfing shorts, pants, t-shirts and footwear in keeping with the trends and fashions of the next fifty seasons. They were all dated, and to be opened in a strict chronological sequence ...

... Which Smokey resolved to follow.

'After all' he thought 'What a disaster to become out of step with the latest styles. A criminal and exile I may be ... but a fashion victim? Not on your Nelly!'

Kipper concluded ...

'Out of the millions of upstanding Muddlehead citizens, you Smokey Kingfish, are only the 102nd lawbreaker alive at the present time. This is not because other lawbreakers have been executed. Not at all. We are not barbarians. No, it is simply that Morningtaria enjoys an almost complete lack of crime!'

Kipper, who as well as Skipper was the only crew member aboard ship, had a jolly red nose and hamster cheeks which bulged out from beneath a large and fluffy white beard.

Smokey sensed that the Skipper was a kind man ... a disposition which was curiously at odds with the Muddlehead propaganda spouting forth from his gob.

It was obvious, even to stupid Smokey, that Kipper was lying.

Head explosions were, after all, executions without trial and although it was true that crime was virtually non-existent in Morningtaria, this was largely because crime required a break from normal behaviour which in turn required 'imagination' ... a Morningtarian attribute as rare as a hairy fish.

If Smokey had been of a more lucid disposition he might have reflected upon those acquaintances he had made since his fateful solo surf at Turd Cove. They amounted to just two ... Skipper Kipper and the Enforcement Officer. Both had been surprisingly nice, when quite probably they should have been unsurprisingly nasty. It was decidedly fishy, but for Smokey, who did not particularly like fish, hairy or otherwise, that fishiness passed over his head like a shoal of flying kippers.

****

And so it was, just five hours after first sighting Penisle 102, Smokey was sat on its southern shore next to his surfboard and the shipping container which housed his provisions, watching as the SS Bulldog disappeared over the horizon.

Smokey was perplexed.

He was a surfer but the shore onto which he had been set was surf less.

It was a conundrum to be sure, and one which occupied him that first week on the island.

Not that Smokey was inclined to roam in search of waves. In Morningtaria, to do so was illegal and besides, surfers never walked.

They caught the bus or, if they were rich enough, rode in beaten up surf wagons with body rust, big motors and noxious smells emanating from a knee-deep detritus of burger wrappers, beer bottles and cigarette stubs strewn about the passenger seats and floor.

Smokey did not know whether his survival pack included a vehicle.

The Skipper had not mentioned one when reading from the manifest and seeing as Smokey could not figure out how to open the container inside which his goodies were allegedly stored, there was no way for him to find out.

Smokey was so frustrated. There in front of him was a huge horde but no matter how hard he tried, he just could not prise open the container's sealed door to get at them. Poor old Smokey! It was driving him mad. The world around him kept shrinking! Just a week ago, it had encompassed so much! ... Bobo Street ... Turd Cove ... the Universe! But now ... in this place ... it had shrunk not only to the size of an island ... not only to the size of the beach upon which he stood ... but to the uniform dimensions of the large metal box before him.

And beside it he stayed ... hour after pointless hour ... staring at the container ... throwing rocks at it.

CHAPTER FIVE

Gary William munched on a Beach Carrot.

They were tasty eating those Beach Carrots and Gary William, who was a donkey, loved them.

'Yum yum!' he mumbled to himself. 'Beach Carrots are the best!'

Not that Gary William was to know but there was no such vegetable as a Beach Carrot ... but that didn't much matter because Gary William had never seen a real Carrot and besides, if donkeys wanted to refer to Coconuts as Beach Carrots, well what harm was there in that?

Gary William lived on the island of Moonshine along with a thousand other donkeys. They were all descended from the first Moonshine donkeys that had landed along with their missionary master, the Reverend Elijah 'Bandicoot' William a century earlier.

Bandicoot had arrived full of the Lord but had not proved up to the task of converting the native Moonshiners to his God fearing ways. Hardly surprising as it turned out for within six months of his arrival the islanders were all dead, courtesy of the influenza Bandicoot had imported along with his donkeys.

Quite naturally, Bandicoot was devastated and whilst he had no inkling as to the true cause of the Islanders' demise, he was rightly certain it was all down to him.

It was a burden too heavy for one man to endure and sure enough, on the first anniversary of his arrival, Bandicoot took a rope, walked into the jungle, found a tall tree and hanged himself.

But what about the donkeys?

Well they fared rather better. Moonshine, as it turned out, suited them just fine.

Free from their puritanical master, those first arrivals enjoyed the tropical climate and spent many a happy day bonking each other senseless and chomping on exotic grasses and fruits. They even discovered that the curious round husks which fell from the palm trees that lined the beach, if kicked and stamped on, would split open and give a hungry donkey a most tasty snack.

Given their idyllic circumstance, a lack of human control and a penchant for the old rumpy pumpy, it was inevitable the population of Moonshine Donkeys swelled to their present number. They became the island's dominant species and as the years went by, gradually forgot the domestic servitude of their previous existence and came to see themselves as the custodians of Moonshine and masters of all they surveyed.

****

Gary William heard a noise. He lifted his nose out of the Beach Carrot and looked up.

Ahead of him, perhaps one hundred metres along the foreshore, was a strange upstanding creature with only two legs connected to the ground and two thinner ones dangling by its sides.

The creature was throwing rocks at a large metal box.

The last time Gary had found himself on this stretch of beach, over a week ago, neither the container nor the strange creature had been there. Curiosity got the better of Gary and he decided to wander over and say hello.

Gary was not scared because he was the master of all he surveyed.

****

'Bong!'

The sound of rock bouncing off the container door reverberated around Smokey's ears. It was a neat sound ... but scant reward to Smokey in his idle and pointless toil.

He looked down.

'Doh!' No more rocks.

Smokey felt a nudge on his behind. He nearly jumped out of his skin. He swung around and was confronted by a donkey that had managed to creep up unseen behind him and was now nuzzling against Smokey's arse.

The donkey looked up.

'Pleased to meet you' said the donkey.

'My name's Gary William. Fancy a Beach Carrot?'

Of course, Smokey didn't understand Donkey. All he heard was a bray. But the shock of seeing the creature jolted his brain out of its listlessness and into life.

At that moment an idea popped into Smokey's head

'I know!' he thought

'Forget this bloody container! I'll ride this donkey across Penisle 102, to the far coast, to find some waves to ride!'

Just one small step for Smokey but a giant leap for Smokey's mind.

It was inconceivable back in Morningtaria for a surfer to search for waves. There, the thought would never have occurred to him. But here, on the island, it had.

A gradual transformation had begun.

****

Looking inland, beyond the palm-fringed coastal plain, a Volcano sat, Buddha-like, on its island throne.

From where he stood, Smokey could see three of the Volcano's four rounded faces. They were perfectly symmetrical, leading upwards, perhaps eight hundred feet before squaring off to form the rim of a large crater.

Not that Smokey was to know, but the Volcano had lain dormant for thousands of years until, sometime during the last century, it had erupted with such violence, the sides of its rim had blasted clean away, leaving a crater twice its original size.

Whilst there had not been a major eruption since then, the Volcano was certainly still active and occasionally took it upon itself to belch and spew out a bungalow sized boulder. For the most part though, its dark conical merely smouldered in a state of uncomfortable and fitful repose.

Surveying the landscape, Smokey decided the quickest route across his island was inland, cutting through the coastal plain - along one of the numerous dried up stream beds - before climbing up to the Volcano's summit and down the other side.

Without a second thought, Smokey picked up the surfboard he had received along with his identity, tucked it under his arm, jumped on top of Gary William and set off.

****

Smokey's enthusiasm lasted all of five minutes.

Immediately, it had started to rain and as he suffered a water torture of drip-drippings onto a furrowed brow, Smokey began to wish he had never begun his arduous journey.

Soon, the ground became too swampy to ride and Smokey had to dismount his donkey and lead it through the jungle instead.

Poor old Gary William! He had only meant to say hello but now here he was, a slave! It was all very disconcerting but there again, for some strange reason; being ordered about by this weird looking creature seemed a very natural thing for him to be doing.

For Smokey, it was extraordinarily tough going. What with the rain and this stupid donkey. He wondered what ever had possessed him to set out on such as arduous mission.

Even so, to turn back was inconceivable. He was a Morningtarian after all, and the obstinacy and bull-headedness which precipitated from such a dull bunch also lent itself to a rather admirable streak of single-mindedness and determination. In short, Smokey had 'spunk!'

But that was of little comfort. Indeed, if the rain wasn't enough; to make matters worse, as soon as Smokey turned off the beach and into the jungle, he was subjected to an aerial bombardment from a bloodthirsty squadron of chicken-size mosquitoes and sand flies the size of still larger domestic farm animals.

Soon, Smokey's walk no longer resembled a walk, but an exuberant, if not demented, Lupino arm-waving dance, inspired by a desperate, if ultimately unsuccessful attempt to swat away the mosquitoes and sand flies.

It was not only his arms. Smokey's feet were performing as well ... skipping to and fro, here and there ... between the multitude of large red crabs which were making their way back to the sea after a night's foray into the jungle in search of the rotting coconut husks which were strewn about the jungle floor.

Dodging crabs on the jungle floor ... dodging the rain, mosquitoes, sand flies and fresher coconuts from the sky.

Oh yes ... fresh coconuts. Lovely to eat. Not so lovely when they are dropping out of the palm trees all around you with the velocity and destructive capability of a small child nudged off a tall building.

Not that they bothered Gary William. He was a native after all, and immune to such things. Gary's only discomfort came from being yanked this way and that by the surfing leash that Smokey had tied round his neck and from being denied the chance to stop and take advantage of this newly located and bountiful supply of fresh Beach Carrots!

****

Miraculously though, all the twirling, darting and gyrating delivered Smokey and Gary, a mere half hour later, out of the jungle to the base of the Volcano, more or less unscathed.

Smokey looked up. The way was steep-sided and devoid of vegetation.

In places, dusty black ashen ridges had formed by the action of wind and rain. Mostly though, the ash had solidified into fist-size chunks of black pumice rock which created a carpet of extremely unstable screed upon which to climb.

Smokey paused for a few moments to catch his breath. He knew the next part of his trek would be difficult. He looked at Gary William who in turn was staring back at him with a look of resignation emanating from big doleful eyes.

So far the donkey had proved about as useful as a glass of water to a drowning man and what's more Smokey doubted whether the rather bulbous animal would make it up the side of the volcano.

There was only one thing for it. Smokey unhitched the leash from around Gary's neck and with a swift slap to its rump shouted...

'On your way fatty!'

'That's gratitude for you!' harrumphed Gary as he trotted off in the direction of his newly located Beach Carrot patch.

****

Smokey turned back to the volcano.

'Oh well!' he thought to himself

'No giving up now!'

And just like that he was off once more.

****

Poor old Smokey! He had to endure forty more minutes of stumbling, sliding and cursing before finally, hot and exhausted; he crawled over the lip of the crater.

Once there, he did not get up immediately. Smokey was knackered but at the same time a wave of elation swept over him. He had completed half his journey!

If Smokey had been mindful of such things, he might have claimed his reward ... a spectacular 360 degree view of the island, cascading down on all sides into a shimmering, convex ocean.

He didn't.

Instead, his gaze fell immediately below, upon the confusion of steam, rock and sulphur which made up the floor of the crater.

The very fact the crater had a floor and was not a hell's gate of magma was something of a surprise to Smokey, and because he saw that he could walk down into it ... he did.

The inner wall of the crater was steep and treacherous, making it impossible to descend directly. Instead Smokey's route manifested into a downward spiral.

It was time consuming but Smokey felt he was making good progress.

Or at least he did until he passed through a foul smelling mist, emerging some minutes later a mere fifty feet above the crater floor.

The smell, whatever it was, caused Smokey to feel dizzy, so he sat down on a large chunk of lava.

It was a mistake. As soon as the weight was lifted off his feet, Smokey was overcome with tiredness.

Such exertion.

He lay back, closed his eyes, and in an instant ... was gone.

CHAPTER SIX

Sky and sea merged into a canvas of polished black. Smokey paddled out alone, his surfboard cutting a silent swathe through an ebony ocean. He looked back upon a contrasting trail of brilliant white ... the residue of spent waves stretching in an arc around a small low-lying island. He saw no vegetation on that land ... the horizontal relieved only by a smattering of dead trees. Twisted and bleached white by salt and sun, they formed a ghostly silhouette against the forbidding gloom.

At that moment, Smokey's whole being existed only to ride the waves.

Emerging from a heaving horizon, they reared up on the most exposed corner of the island, and sidled down the point, a procession of sea snakes, spitting and hissing at the climax of their long journey.

Those waves ... breaking on that shore, offered Smokey a perfection of surf beyond his imagination.

Smokey was riding a beautiful surfboard. Seven feet long and feather light.

He picked his first wave. Smokey swung his board around and as it felt the surge of water from beneath, it lifted and Smokey, cat-like, sprung to his feet.

His style was aggressive ... befitting of a Morningtarian wave-warrior.

Smokey gouged into the face of the wave and slashed great swathes from its roof. Economy of motion did not figure in his approach. To gain the greatest possible momentum, arms were swung maniacally and his head and body were contorted into the most frightful spine-tweaking positions.

After the ride, as he paddled back out, Smokey grew uneasy. He was alone amidst the awesome power of the elements which were collaborating, on all quarters, to put on a most frightening show. On the horizon, the dark sky broke intermittently to reveal sunbeams made brilliant by the gloom they pierced ... and Witch's fingers of lightning cast spells into a cauldron of mountainous sea beyond the point.

Smokey grew scared ... on the verge of panic ... when quite suddenly, all was calm and a dolphin surfaced by his side.

Quite naturally, Smokey and the dolphin began a conversation and whilst Smokey listened and understood, there was no sound.

'You must seek tranquillity between yourself and the waves' began the dolphin.

'Do not react against their strength because that strength is far superior to your own. The waves have travelled infinite distance to arrive at these shores, and whilst they in turn react to the shallows upon which they bend and break, theirs ultimately is the superior power and eventually they will lay their veil over this and all places.

Seek harmony with those waves Smokey. React as they react and you may learn that through perseverance and untainted knowledge, no problem is insurmountable.'

'But how can I gain the knowledge to ride the waves as they are meant to be ridden?' questioned Smokey.

'In most endeavour' continued the dolphin 'to begin, you must learn from others. Smokey, you learnt to surf in the Morningtarian Surf School. There you gained knowledge of wave riding, but that knowledge was tainted by an element of conditioning.

Every thought, every idea and every skill is built on the foundation of previously gained knowledge. They all contain, to a greater or lesser extent, conditioning. It is only through several ages of experience that a mind is able to put that aside and retain only a pure and untainted knowledge. Then, and only then, can true advances be made in all endeavour.

To ride the waves Smokey, you must unshackle your mind and embrace the waves, for they are the guardians of the untainted knowledge you seek and it is they who will teach you.'

The ideas expressed by the dolphin were not simple and quite beyond normal Muddlehead comprehension. To Smokey, in his dreaming, however, there was no struggle to understand. Those ideas slid just as easy into Smokey's sub-conscious as wild honey into the tum of a tubby brown bear.

Smokey continued to surf, but now he sought a union with the waves upon which he rode and as each turn became successively smoother he found that with less effort, he generated more speed.

But there was something more.

Something far greater, far more thrilling than anything he had encountered on top of a wave.

It lay inside ... inside the tube ... a hallowed place where, within the spiralling turbulence of ocean, a surfer-sized cupboard of tranquillity might exist.

And Smokey found it.

The knowledge of this place was enlightenment itself and it spawned in Smokey a higher understanding of the purest form of surfing and with that understanding, a confidence, which grew with every ride so that for a while he did not care that the waves also grew.

Paddling back out, Smokey continuously had to place himself further offshore as the larger swells reared up in the turbulent waters beyond the point.

Smokey was excited about his new surfing style, and this excitement brushed aside any scepticism he might have felt at being alone in such a gigantic sea.

That was until he looked back towards the island.

In much the same way as a mariner, when making his approach towards harbour on a moonless night judges his position from the lead lights above the quay, Smokey had lined up with the hollowed-out trees on the foreshore. But when he tried to spot them, to his horror, he discovered they had disappeared and all that remained of the island was sinking beneath a tumult of surging foam and flotsam.

For a second, Smokey was bewildered and once again felt the sap of panic rise within him. But once again the dolphin surfaced by his side and upon gazing into its dark eyes and the serenity he saw there, Smokey's anxiety fell away and he recalled ...

'... and eventually, they (the waves) will lay a veil over this and all places.'

... and with that, Smokey and the dolphin at once turned, took off and pulled into a wave so large, it engulfed the island and allowed them to ride, in perfect trim, over land and sea, across the four corners of the globe ... and beyond.

CHAPTER SEVEN

BONK!

Smokey felt a dull thud on the side of his head and was instantly awake. He lay sprawled on the ground. Above him, a thatch of tropical rainforest was immediately obscured by three faces peering down at him. In recognition of Smokey's revival, the faces beamed with smiles of relief.

'Dreadfully sorry about dropping you like that.' piped the oldest face 'it was entirely my fault ... I'm a bit clumsy you know.'

'You don't say!' piped up the youngest face, and quite spontaneously, all three faces hooted with genuine delight at what was patently a running joke of quite long standing!

Now, it just so happened that two of the faces, Smokey recognised.

The oldest belonged to Skipper Kipper the captain of the SS Bulldog, whilst the grin of the Enforcement Officer who had arrested Smokey occupied another. The youngest face, a girl's, was instantly recognisable to Smokey as a face to behold ... for it was beautiful.

The girl was Fanny, the eighteen year old sister of Moose who it transpired was merely posing as a member of that dreaded sub-culture class and was not, as his uniform had first lead Smokey to believe, an Enforcer.

Smokey was told all this as he sat with his three new friends, drinking home-made Zonk, on top of a bamboo fishing platform above the waters of a small lagoon.

The trio had found Smokey more dead than alive inside the crater where, overcome by the intoxicating fumes, he had passed out.

With great difficulty, Kipper, Moose and Fanny had heaved Smokey's comatose form out of the crater, down the Volcano and into the rainforest where he had come too. From there the four of them had trudged through a mosquito infested mangrove swamp before arriving at Smokey's long forgotten destination, the North coast of Penisle 102.

****

Smokey had never been inquisitive in Morningtaria.

Who needed to be when the state had all the answers?

But now, in such strange surroundings and more than certainly prompted by the people sitting beside him on the fishing platform, questions longing for asking began fizzing like Whizzpops on the end of his tongue.

'Kipper, what are you doing here?'
'Moose, why are you all being so kind?'
'Kipper, why did you lecture me about Muddlehead virtues?'

'And Fanny, oh Fanny. Could you ever love me the way I'm sure that I will love you?'

Having lost his inhibitions somewhere between his fifth and sixth cup of Zonk, Smokey asked the first three questions. The fourth he kept to himself.

From the answers, it transpired that Moose, twenty four years old, had sixteen years earlier been a terrified child set adrift in a tiny sailing dinghy with Fanny, his infant sister. It was the final, desperate act of a devoted and loving mother who, upon the realisation that the island where they lived and its entire people were doomed, cast her children upon the mercy of the ocean.

'You see Smokey' Moose continued with his head slightly bowed 'We were the people of Sundown.'

Smokey winced and although he said nothing a wave of revulsion and fear, which overcame all Muddleheads at the very mention of Sundown, swept over him.

Moose recognised this and having understood Smokey's reaction, continued.

'All those years ago, the controlling powers of Morningtaria coveted the island of Sundown for the huge deposit of priceless Noodlestones buried beneath its hills. Our people, who for a hundred lifetimes had lived in peaceful and contented isolation, could not permit the rape of Sundown's hallowed earth and politely told the Muddleheads to go away.'

'We just wanted to be left in peace' exclaimed Moose 'but from the instant of that refusal, our fate was sealed.'

'Those Bosspigs really surpassed themselves. They embarked on a smear campaign. It turned the Muddleheads' thoughts towards us from indifference to a fear verging on hysteria. Sundown became 'The Island of Flesh Eaters' whose ghoulish inhabitants, upon dark, changed into grotesque flying demons with raven's wings, who crossed the channel separating our shores and descended on peaceful neighbourhoods to feast on the tender flesh of Muddlehead children plucked from their beds.'

'When the Bosspigs announced the successful invasion of Sundown and the subsequent extermination of The Sundowners ...'

Moose stood up and confronted Smokey with a fixed stare.

'... Was it any wonder you and your kin jumped and hooted for joy?'

Moose sat down, bowed his head and exhaled a poignant sigh, before concluding.

'Smokey, when I mentioned who I was, it was clear from your expression that you were a child who feared the dark shadows at your window.'

Smokey said nothing.

He merely sat in silence, eyes fixed on Moose ... a study of concentration ... scanning Moose's whole anatomy for any visible sign of Raven's plumage.

He saw none and with no small amount of hesitation concluded that he was not about to become dinner.

It was all very ... very confusing.

It was night time after all ... and contrary to what Smokey had thought possible, he was sitting next to a Sundowner who retained a human skin. Smokey, who had always believed everything he was told, suddenly couldn't. Contradiction was not a word contained in the Muddlehead dictionary, but Muddlehead teachings and Moose's story conspired to form exactly that.

Smokey decided to ask a question.

'Moose, how did you and Fanny survive being set adrift ?'

Moose's expression suddenly brightened ... and with an affectionate sideways glance at the chubby old man with the red cheeks and white beard, who having drunk rather too many Zonks, was snoring away contentedly in the corner, replied.

'It was Kipper. He picked us up and brought us to Moonshine. He took care of us and we have lived here ever since.'

Smokey interrupted 'so this isn't Penisle 102 then...it's Moonshine!' ... and afterwards felt quite amazed at the succinct deduction he had made.

'No and then yes!' laughed Fanny.

With her reply, the girl gave Smokey such a warm, affectionate smile that he felt compelled to lower his face in a coy attempt to hide his blushes.

She continued 'it was part of a telling that we hoped would prompt a questioning on your part. You see, we had to weave a story that was so full of holes, even a Muddlehead might see through it.'

Fanny's features grew harder. 'We need you to see things for what they are, not for what they seem. The Bosspigs for example. On your journey here, the Skipper led you to believe that the Bosspigs had spared you ... had sentenced you not to death, but exile. Did you not question that ? Well, it is for us to tell you now that after riding that solo wave in Turd Cove, your head was a second from being exploded, courtesy of an Enforcer on beach patrol. However, at the very instant of raising and aiming his 'Boofhead', he was dealt a sympathetically light blow on the back of his own head, rendering him unconscious, rendering Moose a new Enforcer's Uniform ... and saving your life.'

She continued, 'It was a miracle we happened upon you when we did and straight away we knew we had to get you away as quickly as possible. If not ... if you had been left to your own devices, you would have been caught and ...'

Moose finished the sentence '... you would have been exterminated ... just like the Sundowners.'

In speaking so plainly, Moose betrayed his suspicion towards all Muddleheads. It was deep seated but over time, Moose, with the help of Kipper and the affection of Fanny, his younger sister, had almost entirely rid him of the bitterness and frustration which had been his burden since the loss of his parents in the massacre of the

Sundowners. At the time, a passionate loathing, like the volcanic island of Moonshine itself, had risen from the sea depths of his soul. Moose's coolness toward Smokey was merely a faint echo of what, just a few years previous, had been an all consuming hate towards the Muddleheads.

****

Inevitably though, Moose's nobility, coupled with the healing properties of time and love, would cause in him an affection towards Smokey to develop so that in the passing of just a few weeks, the one would look upon the other not as a Muddlehead, but as a brother.

****

"GRNNNNTTT!" The conversation on the fishing platform was interrupted by Kipper who had begun to snore extremely loudly.

Fanny, whose sparkling eyes betrayed a mischievous intent, sidled over to the comatose lump. Once up close, she clamped Kipper's nostrils shut with one hand and with the other, blocked his mouth.

Immediately, Kipper gagged; his eyelids flew open and the confusion of one whose slumber has been nipped in the bud was evident and amusing for all to see. Fanny and Moose giggled and a drowsy grin spread across the Skipper's face as he pulled himself up and with outstretched arms and bulging belly, enjoyed a tumultuous yawn.

Then ... inevitably ... his eyes fell on the half full jug of Zonk.

The Skipper reached over, grabbed the jug, poured out four full cups and keeping one for himself passed the other three to Smokey, Moose and Fanny.

'Not so fast!' Kipper rebuked as Moose lifted his cup and went to take a drink.

'Its Flamey time!'

Moose went first and with minimal fuss, struck a light; ignited his drink; raised the cup and smoothly swallowed its contents as an alcohol fuelled flame danced barely a flea's length from his lips.

Fanny employed the same controlled technique ... and Smokey too.

That just left the Skipper who with the know-it-all expression of a past master, grabbed at the cup, thrust it to his lips and like a stranded goldfish gaping at the sky, attempted to swallow the flaming elixir with a series of convulsive gulps.

Disastrously, the Zonk began to trickle down Kipper's chin closely followed by the searing blue flame.

Kipper panicked and jerked the cup away from his lips with such haste the contents did not have time to follow and ended up all over his shirt. As both his chin and upper torso ignited, Kipper jumped up and frantically began to tear around the fishing platform, pawing at the flames which by now were engulfing him. Finally, he tripped on a protruding piece of bamboo and fell headlong into the dark waters of the lagoon ten feet below.

Smokey darted to the edge of the platform and called out to Kipper who was nowhere to be seen. At a loss, he turned back to Moose and Fanny. They were no help whatsoever. In fact, much to Smokey's consternation, they were rolling around on the floor in hysterics ... with tears of laughter streaming down their cheeks. Smokey began waving his arms around and generally working himself up into a frightful panic. He started gibbering 'OOH! OOH! He's gonna drown! He's gonna drown! Do something! DO SOMETHING!'

Moose and Fanny, who by now were in a completely helpless state, could only babble and hoot in reply.

Disgusted, Smokey resolved to take matters into his own hands. He turned and jumped headlong off the fishing platform in pursuit of Kipper. It was a rather heroic course of action but also entirely unnecessary for as it turned out, Kipper had survived the flames and the fall entirely unscathed. That much was plain for Smokey to see ... a bat-like Smokey who upon launching himself off the platform had caught his foot on a loose end of rope and found himself dangling upside-down; his nose barely inches from the water.

... And it was from this embarrassing position that he spotted Kipper floating contentedly on his back beneath the platform.

Although just a few seconds had passed from the time of his fall, Kipper had already returned to a deep slumber which a perplexed Smokey recognised from the familiar snores and grunts emanating from the bulbous old fellow.

Perhaps it should have occurred to Smokey how very strange it was that the Skipper could so happily spend the night sleeping in the ocean. Moose and Fanny, having recovered sufficiently from the giggles, had explained to Smokey ... after they had hauled him back onto the platform, sat him down and given him a nice hot cup of Cocoa ... that Kipper rarely slept on land.

... and that was all the explanation needed, for Smokey, who coincidentally had slept on his own 'Muddlesnuggle' waterbed back in Morningtaria, did not think to question this peculiar practise, for he himself was tired and more than ready for a nice long kip.

After Smokey had finished his Cocoa, Fanny, sensing his tiredness, suggested they all turn in for the night.

She got up and Smokey watched as she crossed the platform to a large wooden chest from which she retrieved three blankets.

Fanny knew she was being watched and it made her feel strangely uneasy. She had first set eyes on Smokey that fateful day in Turd Cove and now it was for the benefit of this stranger that she found herself growing more than a little self-conscious ... checking all motion and carrying herself with a feline grace both uncommon to her but at the same time natural and easy.

Smokey was captivated.

Later, when his body screamed for sleep, Smokey's mind was a confusion of images. He lay on top of his bedding, for the still night was stifling. As he strained to see the outline of Fanny, asleep on the far side of the platform, he conjured up stories ... imaginative stories, all of which were varied in landscape and situation, but nonetheless uniform in their outcome ... a climax where he and Fanny, at last, turned to one another and with eyes full of wantonness ... embraced.

CHAPTER EIGHT

Skipper Kipper snored but he wasn't asleep.

Earlier, he had been jolly, but now ... floating in starry reflection on the dark and glassy water, Kipper felt lonesome.

His old body was giving out ... had been for a long time and whilst he couldn't replace it ... Kipper could leave it ... could leave then return ... time and time again.

That night, Kipper left to be with Watersplash.

As the lagoon fell silent ... as Fanny, Moose and Smokey slept ... Kipper submerged and swam effortlessly, arcing through the shallows, out through the lagoon and into the depths of the open ocean beyond.

****

Watersplash had perished ... had smashed against Morningtaria ... and the Muddleheads. But Watersplash was a mere foot soldier ... just as past and future Watersplashes were and would become. They were all new suns ... distinguished by the day upon which they shone ... but still ... the one same sun. As was Watersplash the one same wave ... distinguishable only by the space and time he filled. One wave but an army of infinite waves.

Watersplashes all ... but all one Watersplash.

Watersplash's meeting with Kipper acted as a pick-me-up. Watersplash was weary. He had been on a long journey, had travelled great distance to a far off destination and was now returned.

At the farthest point ... at the last frontier ... he had pushed just a little further ... had turned then headed for home ... a backwash of ever decreasing circumference ... headed back to the place from where he had begun. Headed back home with a gift ... with knowledge of all that had come before ... knowledge to pass on ... to help smooth the way.

Only now ... upon his return ... did he know it had not been for nothing.

Not so long as it ended beneath the feet of a surfer called Smokey Kingfish.

But that would have to wait. Smokey wasn't quite ready for Watersplash. It was Kipper's job to make him so. The Skipper knew this and knew just what needed to be done. Smokey needed protection and inspiration ... and the Skipper, as angel and muse ... could provide both.

CHAPTER NINE

The following days and weeks flew by.

During this time, Smokey grew more and more attached to his new family.

Happy times were spent surfing and fishing with Moose. The two became quite inseparable and Moose delighted in teaching Smokey the various skills and techniques of island living. Moose was a stylish surfer, a cunning fisherman and an expert and patient craftsman of wood, copra, coral and all those abundant Moonshine commodities which might be sculptured and carved to make important things like outrigger canoes, fishing tackle and surfboards.

In turn, Smokey was besotted with Moose.

He trailed him everywhere, even copied his mannerisms, like the way Moose cursed under his breath when a fish broke his line or when he missed a particularly good wave.

Smokey was inspired by the simplicity and common sense with which Moose conducted himself. Most everything had a reason, a routine and a 'knack'.

Even so, Moose was often quite spontaneous, even rash. Maybe it was more a release than anything and such 'episodes' took place only during times of leisure when they were of little consequence beyond the immediate danger they might present to Moose himself.

Often, he would surf the angriest of seas on a small wave 'zippy-stick', so wobbly it gave him next to no chance of remaining upright. Smokey, who sat in the safety of the channel on such days, would cover his eyes rather than watch those hideous waves conspire with devious reef to bludgeon Moose into a pulp. Upon the crest of such beasts, Moose, having no chance of making the takeoff, would employ the zippy-stick as a springboard from which to launch into a freefall dive. To Smokey, he appeared to be racing with the guillotine curl of the wave ... racing to be the first to smash headlong into the reef. It was bone-chilling stuff to be sure, but time and again Moose survived, emerging from the water, sometimes walking, sometimes crawling and bloody, but always smiling.

Smokey was quick to learn any lesson taught ... the Muddlehead resistance to change and ideas new, falling from him like a redundant snakeskin. He was happy to try anything and Moose was willing to teach him everything.

Well almost ...

There was a regular time when Moose insisted Smokey did not follow. On those occasions, Moose and Kipper disappeared to the farthest edge of the reef. There, where the knee-deep turquoise of the lagoon fell into the deep blue of the channel, Moose and Kipper partook in the ancient art of Octopus Luring.

Octopus was a delicacy enjoyed throughout the vast archipelago of Wallynesia of which Moonshine and Sundown were a part.

In all the populated islands, Octopus was revered and the method of its capture followed strict ceremony ... especially when undertaken for the first time, when it promised a successful hunter the rite of passage into adulthood.

Moose and the Skipper loved Octopus Luring.

They would happily prowl for hours along the edge of the reef, peering into the depths directly below them.

Where the coral cliff face dropped away, Octopus lay in wait, ready to embrace their next meal.

A fearful aura surrounded those creatures. For generations, seafaring folk had told tale of mysterious becalming in strange seas where neither bird circled nor fish breached ... of ominous silence followed at once by a churning of the sea made so from on deep ... of bow and beam lurching ... of the spellbound peering overboard, choice neither known nor made to stay put or to run ... fate offering no such choice to death touched souls plucked screaming from the swaying deck by hideous tentacles.

But that was for the storybooks.

All that concerned Moose and the Skipper was the sport ... plus the delicious prospect of a jolly good feed!

With that in mind, every couple of weeks, the pair would set out across the reef and what transpired went something like this ...

Once a likely looking spot was found, Moose and Kipper would prepare for the luring. Strong footholds were located and the lure smeared with smelly fish oil and bound in a thick copra rope.

With everything ready, the two figures would move forward to the edge of the coral. Kipper would take a vice-like grip on one end of the rope, place his feet carefully and assume the pose of one about to commence a tug o' war contest. At that same moment, Moose who as it turned out was himself the lure, would step off the reef and plummet like a sack of kittens and stones into the channel.

As was often the case, an octopus of rather single-minded disposition would spring from his crafty hideout to claim his free lunch. Inevitably, he would become rather confused for although that lunch was cradled securely in his eight arms and there was no struggle, he would feel an irresistible pull towards the strange waterless world above his head.

Now, it must be said that Octopus are stubborn creatures. They are also quite frugal and hate seeing good food go to waste. Bearing this in mind, it is little wonder that come hell or low water, said 'puss would never consider letting go of that heaven sent morsel in the rather fetching shorts ... and that, sure as burps follow beer, was a mistake. Before he might conclude that there was no such thing as a free lunch, he would be plucked from the water and prised off the object of his initial desire. Finally, as he lay stranded in an alien environment, as he caught sight of a large rock moving swiftly towards his head, the poor 'puss would have an apocalyptic revelation that the tables had indeed been turned and the only lunch to be served that particular day, was him!

It is, perhaps, morbid to look at things from the poor squidgy creatures' point of view. By far the happier image is of the four friends, Smokey, Fanny, Moose and Kipper later that evening, feasting on a mouth-watering dish of Octopus Kebab marinated in coconut milk and washed down with a copious amount of Kipper's specially formulated Zonk.

Whilst the Octopus that Moose and Kipper caught were not of the dimensions described in fishy seafarers' tales, they did, nonetheless, provide for Octopus based lunch and dinner for at least a week thereafter.

Fanny's culinary dexterity always proved a marvel. Octopus Curry might follow Octopus Pie as in turn it had followed the Octopus Kebab. By the week's end, as Fanny added the final morsels to, say, a light and fluffy Octopus Soufflé it was always an extraordinary resolve that prevented Smokey, Moose and Kipper from screaming in unison... 'NOT FLAMIN' OCTOPUS AGAIN!'

****

Aside from Octopus Luring, there were other times that Smokey did not spend with Moose.

They were spent with Fanny.

He often saw her gathering tender kelps and waded out to help carry the palm-frond basket she filled. It was an excuse to be with her and equally, Fanny enjoyed his company. During these times, Smokey would snatch tentative glances at Fanny whenever he sensed she would not notice. The honey-brown skin of her arm, glistening as it emerged from a rock pool. Her waist and hips so slim and yet so curvaceous, swinging provocatively when the girl accidentally stepped on a sharp shell. Smokey marvelled at these things in silence and in his mind, they lingered so that in the midst of conversation his awkward stammers and replies were a give-away to Fanny. She in turn was transparent in her response to Smokey's more outstanding gaffes ... letting out a giggle, covering her mouth with her hand and dropping her head in mild shame that she had let slip the delicious façade.

Those daily liaisons between Smokey and Fanny slowly, inevitably wound a course towards a final play where pursuer lays open his hand to the pursued.

It happened one morning when Smokey engineered a chance meeting with Fanny as the latter gathered Scooberries on the fertile lower slope of the Volcano's Northern face.

His excuse, a hike to the far side of Moonshine to collect those supplies which had accompanied his arrival on the island one month previous.

Smokey and Fanny greeted and sat down together on the soft grass.

Conversation began but was forced. After an uncomfortable pause, Smokey, head hung low, reached over and took Fanny by the hand. He fixed a stare at that hand and did not dare raise his eyes towards Fanny's for fear of the rejection he might see.

Smokey need not have worried for as he sat there, his whole body shaking with nervous excitement, Fanny accepted his hand, drew it slowly from the grass and placed it softly against her cheek. She turned towards Smokey and her emerald eyes met his, drawing them, siren like, into the depths of her innermost thoughts ... where he saw her own desires reflecting back at his.

Without letting go of Fanny's hand, Smokey stood up and in the same movement drew her up so that they stood facing each other. He did not stop looking into Fanny's eyes as he moved his hands down to the hem of her dress. He took it between thumb and forefinger and dragged it upwards over contours of thigh, hip, waist and arm until it was unhitched, leaving only the slender, vulnerable and entirely naked form of a beautiful young woman.

Smokey wore only his shorts. They had barely disguised the dull ache in his loins and now, as he felt his legs grow wobbly he had to lift and unhook them before they fell harmlessly to the ground.

Fanny, her eyes all the time fixed on Smokey's, let herself slip down his body until she was crouched in front of him. He could feel her cool breath against his skin and he gave an involuntary gasp. Now the temptress, Fanny, realising the effect, gave Smokey the naughtiest of looks and revealed that seductive posture for the tease it was by moving instead to Smokey's shorts which she gathered up, folded and placed neatly on top of a Scooberry Bush for safe keeping.

But Smokey was not for playing games.

He rushed and pulled her to him. In turn, Fanny, who felt his urgency, bowed her head and nestled it tight to the curve of his neck. His hands fell to her buttocks and in turn she stroked his rib cage before slender fingers slid between naked tummies and down to that which she yearned to be inside her.

Smokey pulled Fanny to the floor. She sank beneath the tall grass and its tender, moist shoots felt cool against her flushed skin. Finally, he moved onto her. He prised her slender legs out from under his own until fully exposed, she arched her back and thrust forward to accept him.

CHAPTER TEN

Colonel Conga had been assigned a new case ... the case of the missing Smokey. He had received the brief directly from his father ... who was a Bosspig.

Conga was a Chief Enforcement Officer. He was born a Bosspig, but had chosen, for the time being at least, not to invoke his membership. This was not because he disliked the Bosspigs ... or the power that came from being one. On the contrary ... he loved power, but Conga's preferred brand was decidedly more 'hands on'. Being an Enforcer gave him that power, particularly within the intimate surrounds of an interrogation room where Conga could be alone with a steady supply of Morningtaria's wrongdoers.

The Colonel loved to extract colourful confessions from the poor souls who crossed his path and he was ably assisted in the performance of this delightful duty by a most prized possession ... his Tool Box.

Conga was a talented and imaginative interrogator and the knick-knacks and gadgets contained in that unassuming little box gave him the edge over each and every one of his rivals in the Department of the Chief Enforcers.

It was Conga's proud boast that the contents of his Box were entirely of his own design and construction. They were his babies ... all invaluable to his work ... and he was meticulous when it came to their upkeep. Every blade was shiny and sharp; every clamp and crusher freshly greased; and not a stray bit of fluff could be found on his patent Electrified Testicle Socks.

****

Conga immediately set to work on the case of the missing Smokey.

He centred his investigation on the Surf Beach. Kingfish's rule breach and subsequent apprehension by a man posing as an Enforcement Officer had been captured on film by a Dobberman.

The Dobbermen, a particularly odious group, roamed the streets and ghettos of Morningtaria in dirty, smelly raincoats which concealed hidden surveillance cameras. Dobbermen frequented bars, brothels and Bingo Halls and any interesting film they took within the confines of those seething, amoral cesspits was passed on to the Bosspigs who in turn were happy to allow the Dobbermen free reign to enjoy their more depraved pleasures without fear of persecution.

Although they never would have admitted it, the Bosspigs saw the Dobbermen as kindred spirits and clandestine interaction between the two Clubs was common.

****

Despite the images captured on the Dobberman's film and despite his rigorous and expert efforts, Conga had nothing to go on.

The investigation was proving to be a thorn in his side. Nobody had come forward with information as to the whereabouts of Smokey Kingfish and because of this, the Colonel had quickly concluded that nobody knew anything.

It was a reasonable conclusion.

After all, there was no discretion or loyalty amongst the Muddleheads and wrongdoers were almost always 'grassed up' by somebody they knew.

The Bosspigs had seen to that.

It was simply a case of taking capital from the Muddlehead's love of something for nothing. They loved Prizes and the Bosspigs controlled the Prize supply.

Everybody dobbed someone in if they thought they might get their sweaty paws on a Prize. Simple folk dobbed on their friends for a box seat at Friday night Bongoball. Even little Johnny dobbed on Granny for a dozen 'JackShite' half price 'BogBurger' tokens and whilst he stuffed his face, the poor old dear would be dragged, kicking and screaming down to a local Enforcer's Office, to have her cake hole sewn up for allegedly calling Chief Bertie Bosspig a 'fat poof' when he appeared on the telly!

Was it any wonder Morningtaria's 'Big Prize Crime Line' rang hotter than all the Continent's saucy sex lines put together?

With one exception.

Unfortunately for the Colonel, it did not ring with news of Smokey Kingfish.

No leads were forthcoming. The Enforcer who had been relieved of his uniform by Moose had been of no help. Conga, within the confines of his interview room had tried to jog that poor officer's memory but due to an unfortunate power surge ... had fried it instead.

By now, almost two months had passed since Smokey's disappearance and the case had become the Colonel's obsession. Every spare moment, he agonised over the whereabouts of Kingfish and his mysterious saviour ... and sat for hours studying the Dobberman's surveillance film for any clue ... but to no avail.

Finally, in an act of desperation, Conga had the computer enhanced surveillance film circulated amongst his staff ... and the Dobbermen.

It was a loathsome act for Conga. Personally, he was repelled by the Dobbermen and to him, it felt like admitting defeat ... placing his hopes in whatever 'that scum might come up with.' But ever the pragmatist, Conga admitted that it was all that was left for him to do.

CHAPTER
ELEVEN

If, the day he had interrupted Fanny and her Scooberries, Smokey had indeed ventured to the far side of the island to collect his supplies ... and if he had taken a crowbar to prise open the door ... he would have discovered the shipping container was empty.

Smokey had never questioned the Skipper's assertion that the large metal box had been full to the brim with goodies. It had however somewhat flummoxed him weeks earlier to discover that it was locked. To Smokey, it was a conundrum to be sure ... but only one in a series of conundrums designed to make him ponder over the strangeness of his situation.

All a part of the learning process.

The container had been empty ... but that was not always the case.

Kipper, Fanny and Moose often used it to carry cargo.

A couple of years previous, with a rusty old freighter the Skipper had won in a game of chance; they had started a coastal haulage business.

The venture made the trio a small return but more important, for Kipper at least, it allowed them unquestioned access to Morningtaria.

The Skipper undertook trips to that ignorant land more out of curiosity than anything ... because he was interested to see how things changed over time.

Not much.

Or not that was until Smokey sauntered into Turd Cove that fateful morning.

Maybe it had or maybe it hadn't been a tremendous fluke that Kipper, Moose and Fanny, who had arrived off the boat from Moonshine an hour earlier, had been strolling along the Promenade the precise moment Smokey went 'Sole Surfing'. Whatever, they had taken a tremendous risk extracting Smokey ... especially Moose who had spotted the Enforcer on the beach with his standard issue 'Boofhead' already raised and trained at Smokey's head, and without hesitation had sprung into action.

Moose had leapt off the sea wall, bounded down the beach and flattened the unsuspecting plod. He had bundled the man into a beach hut, had stripped him and emerged less than a minute later, wearing the Enforcer's uniform.

By that time, the Skipper and Fanny, realising it was best they were not around, had disappeared down a side street and into the city.

That just left Moose to conduct a fake arrest, frogmarch Smokey off the beach, bundle him into the back of the first open car he came across ... hotwire the thing ... and make for the harbour.

Whilst the Skipper had got the lad away on the next sailing, Moose and Fanny had stayed. Brother and sister had spent a tiring few days hitching the five hundred miles North, to Cape Cow, where they had cadged a lift on a fishing boat across the fifty mile passage back to Moonshine.

Kipper had not allowed them to sail with him ... or go near the ship whilst it was in port. Far too risky. The Skipper had known the vessel was liable to be boarded and searched by the Enforcers who, he had rightly guessed, were in an investigative frenzy after the unprecedented assault on one of their colleagues.

Kipper knew they might have leads and he did not want his 'children' on board if Smokey was traced. If the Enforcers found him, everybody on the ship would be for the chop. That was how it was in Morningtaria where the justice system was founded on the age old Lupin dictum ... 'Invicinitum Invishitum'.

****

That was two months ago.

A lot had happened since then.

And now, for the first time since Smokey's arrival on Moonshine, Moose, big brother to Fanny and hero to Smokey, ventured back to Morningtaria ... alone.

He had casually dropped the question to Kipper as the old man sat stirring a boiling pot of Zonk.

Might he make the journey single-handed? Moose had asked ... expecting a point blank refusal.

After all it was The Skipper's ship and it was The Skipper whose insistence that Moose and Fanny never leave his side whilst in Morningtaria that caused Moose to suspect that Kipper did not trust him to stay out of trouble.

'The mere fact that Kipper had left us after we rescued Smokey, did not change things' thought Moose.

'It was just on that particular occasion, he had no choice.'

It was somewhat of a surprise, therefore, when without so much as raising an eyebrow, Kipper who continued to stir the fermenting Zonk with his left hand, took the Skipper's cap from off his head with the right and handed it to Moose.

Kipper knew that Moose had to go.

****

What did that weathered old duffer know?

He knew that things had changed.

It had been inevitable. Smokey's arrival had seen to that. As for Moose ? Well, Kipper sensed a change in him too.

As a lad, Moose had exercised a dark and fearful temper. A head full of demons. They had fed off his frustrations, filling a void created by the loss of his parents. Over the years though, the Skipper's patience and affection had pacified Moose and the young man had learnt to control those demons. Kipper knew how much of a struggle it was for Moose. It was as if the whole of him was engaged in a constant struggle to keep the darkness at bay. The Skipper knew that Moose best achieved this by going surfing. It had a cleansing effect. He only had to paddle out to the waves crashing on the outer reefs ; only had to feel the surge of water beneath his board and upon his return, it seemed to Kipper as if all Moose's torments were washed clean away.

For Moose's part, he had not been aware of the growing feelings between his sister and Smokey.

Initially, he had fought to confound his animosity towards the young Morningtarian and during those first few weeks had even grown fond of him. It had been easy. They had shared so many good times.

But that was before he had come across Smokey and his sister in the Scooberry bushes.

Then, Moose had struggled to contain his rage, had turned and ran.

Smokey and Fanny had been oblivious to his presence which had indeed been fortunate for if at that moment Smokey had looked up from his lovemaking, with one glance he may have prompted the hatred which at that moment was burning in Moose's eyes to manifest itself into murder.

It would have been easy to reason that Moose's hatred towards Smokey came as a result of an over-protective nature. Moose cared deeply for Fanny and looked out for her as any big brother might. But Moose's hatred did not grow from that encounter. No ... it had always been there. It was one half of Moose's whole being and Smokey's fondness for Fanny had merely summoned it to the fore. The hatred was evil and did not need reason to take control of Moose's spirit ... just a prompt.

From that day on, Moose avoided Smokey. Every other evening, he found reason to stay away from the fishing platform. Moose wandered aimlessly along the beaches of Moonshine, often until midnight, snacking on coconut and dried fish so as to avoid the communal supper. For his part, Smokey did not seem to notice for he was too preoccupied with Fanny.

But Kipper noticed. He knew what was happening but equally, knew the futility of intervention.

Moose's hatred grew so strong, so overwhelming that he could no longer bring himself to conduct civil conversation, even with the Skipper. He would snipe, he would antagonise, so it was best, Kipper decided, to leave well alone.

And so Moose was left pretty much to his own devices. But as time went on, the hatred in him did not subside, but grew and festered until any goodness remaining in Moose was all but eaten away ... leaving only a desire to have done with the whole sorry affair by having done with Smokey.

Evil imagination worked swiftly then, and soon Moose had conceived of a plan ...

****

Smokey still wanted to join Moose and Kipper on their fortnightly trip to the far side of the lagoon. He felt he wouldn't have the respect afforded real men until he had lured an Octopus.

Smokey had talked about it with Fanny and although she had tried her utmost to turn him off the idea - for she knew the terrible risks involved - Smokey was determined to one day carry out the ritual. He did not think this would be soon because it was something that Moose would have to help him with and Moose never seemed to be around much anymore.

In the short time Smokey had resided on Moonshine he had learnt how to fish, and his natural surfing talent had come to fruition outside the restraints of Turd Cove.

He was not, however, ready for Octopus luring.

Smokey hadn't trained for it ... hadn't run on the seabed carrying boulders to build up his lungs ... hadn't learned to wrestle an Octopus with only his teeth.

Smokey did not know he was meant to know these things but even if he had, if given the opportunity to go Octopus Luring, he still would have jumped at the chance.

And that is exactly what he did when early one morning Moose emerged from the jungle, stole up to the fishing platform and whilst Fanny and the Skipper slept, ushered Smokey to come with him to the far side of the Lagoon.

****

Smokey had learned to question things which didn't appear quite right ... like why he and Moose now ventured out to the far side of the lagoon, in search of Octopus, without Kipper. He asked the question to himself, but not to Moose because he didn't want to risk the chance that Moose had merely overlooked the absence of the Skipper and if so reminded, would turn back, thus causing Smokey to miss out on possibly his one and only chance of Octopus luring.

If only that were the case.

When they arrived at the chosen place, Moose quickly prepared. He didn't bother to check the rope ... or to look for likely footholds.

What was the point?

He offered Smokey only a token explanation of what the luring involved before binding the petrified lad and booting him unceremoniously off the precipice into the dark waters of the channel.

Smokey sank some five metres before passing a crevice cut deep into the coral cliff face which was home to a large Octopus who went by the name of Bert.

Bert had just returned from a long night's revelry with some Scallops on the seabed. He was worn out. He wasn't at all hungry but when Smokey passed before his eyes, all trussed up like a Bosspig in a Bingo Hall, Bert couldn't quite help himself and out of his lair he shot.

Smokey, whose arms were tightly secured, was helpless, and as Bert's tentacles pressed at his rib cage, he felt the air squeeze from his lungs like the last delicious slither of Chubbee Cheeze from a deflated Chubbee Cheeze tube. Smokey's last image, as he was drawn into Bert's Cave, before losing consciousness was of a rope-end , the one that should have been attached to Moose's hand, sinking aimlessly into the depths.

Moose himself had viewed the whole sorry episode from above. He had peered down through crystal water; had seen the helpless Smokey dragged into darkness; had turned and walked away, his conspiracy complete.

But something made him stop ... made Moose scream with exasperation ... turn again, run and dive headlong into the lagoon after his victim.

Moose swam down and into Bert's hideaway where he caught the Octopus unawares, nibbling on Smokey's big toe. Moose sunk his knife into the tentacle which Bert had wrapped, like a coiled snake, around the teenager's neck and hacked away at its rubbery flesh until Bert's eight arms became seven. It was frightfully painful for Bert but he was in no fit state to defend himself. He was still feeling pretty knackered from the previous night's debauchery and the only resistance he was able to offer came in the form of a rather sad and pathetic ink fart.

Moose wrenched Smokey free, grabbed him around the waist and pulled his limp body out and up towards the surface.

Moose had to drag himself up onto the reef before he could lift Smokey to safety. Then he performed a textbook resuscitation and as Smokey, who had quite miraculously returned to life, sat on a rock alternately sobbing and puking, Moose without so much as a word, turned once more and walked away.

He left Moonshine the very next day.

CHAPTER TWELVE

What was the cause of Moose's change of heart?

Why had he returned to Smokey?

Moose agonised over these and other questions as he sat toying with his empty glass.

The bar was crowded. It was Bongoball night and the regulars at the Tipsy Turd were boozing it up big time in front of the screen. Cecil Gonad had just scored a 'Squelcher', his fifth of the game. Cecil was the Golden Boy and a Squelcher was a top drawer score. The crowd packed into The Bongobowl erupted ... the crowd in the Tipsy Turd did likewise. Moose just burped and muttered something relating to Bongoball supporters and the physiological anomalies resulting from their sisters and mothers being one and the same person.

Moose was drunk and his mutterings were just loud enough to attract the attention of a rather large fellow in a Biff BC shirt sitting beside him.

Bubba Biff was not the most intelligent of individuals but he did have a passion for Bongoball and especially Biff BC. Bubba's identity, among other things, was that of 'Fan' and he took the role seriously, so much so in fact, that he had recently changed his name in honour of his favourite team, the team which, incidentally, had just scored.

Now, Bubba was confused and this confusion lasted for approximately twenty seconds which was the time it took him to ascertain that the fellow sitting to his left was not a Biff BC supporter.

Bubba manoeuvred his face in front of Moose's

'What you say, boy?'

Bubba slurred the question ... not because he was drunk but because he was rather stupid and found the skill of stringing more than two words together a bit complicated.

If Moose had been his usual lucid self he might have recognised this, in which case he almost certainly could have distracted Bubba with enough sophisticated patter to make good his escape.

Instead, Moose countered with a simple two word ... two syllable refrain.

'Up yours!' was elementary enough even for Bubba's snail pace cognition and his response did not require much in the way of brain power, just a forward jerk of the neck to deliver unto Moose a lightning fast head butt which caused the latter's nose to splatter across his face like so much road kill across a highway. As Moose fell back, Bubba followed through with a swift combination to the stomach and kidney causing Moose to drop to the floor where next he felt the size twelve boot on Bubba's right foot plant his face squarely against the beer soaked linoleum.

Bubba may not have had much upstairs, but his years spent in the meanest Muddlehead bars and on the violent terraces of The Bongobowl had moulded him into a dirty and dangerous street fighter.

Bubba was a product of precise Bosspig conditioning ... a patriotic zombie whose identity was easily switched from Fan to Soldier ... to Enforcer.

But more on the Soldiering.

Bubba was a veteran. He had served during the invasion of Sundowner, and on his forearm were tattooed twenty seven one inch vertical lines ... being one for every Sundowner man, women and child Bubba had fought and killed during that 'heroic' campaign.

Bubba certainly was not a man to trifle with.

Meanwhile, back in the Tipsy Turd, whilst Moose was spread-eagled on the floor impersonating a Wallynesian Dance Mat, a decidedly Muddleheaded reaction occurred.

The clientele that evening was a potentially volatile mix of Biff BC and Rumble Rovers fans and each group looked upon Moose and Bubba quite differently. What the Rumble Rovers crowd saw was a big buffoon in a Biff BC shirt merrily laying into some floor-residing unfortunate who they could only conclude to be one of their own number.

On the other side of the coin, the Biff BC supporters saw their compatriot, Bubba, enjoying a great sporting moment at the expense of some Rumble lowlife.

Instantaneously, Rumbles and Biffs moved en masse to offer assistance to either Moose or Bubba and what followed was a five minute cartoon sketch of dust clouds, flying fists and feet. Bar stools were wrapped around heads ; Bubba's were biffed and Moose's mangled. It was all jolly good fun and everybody in the Tipsy Turd joined in with gusto.

Everybody that was except the Dobberman, Percy Snivel, who sat in a quiet corner of the bar, panning the scene with his hidden camera.

Percy thought he recognised Moose.

Hadn't he seen his photo recently?

He wasn't sure. Percy always remembered a face but Moose's, at that particular moment, was rather swollen and bloody.

Just then, a patrol of Enforcers burst through the door. Immediately, they joined the fray so that at first, the dust cloud simply grew larger and flying batons were added to the fists and feet. Slowly though, the dust subsided to reveal a large number of dazed and unconscious fans slumped over tables and propped up against the piss pots under the bar.

At that stage, the Enforcement officers, having enjoyed themselves immensely, turned to leave. Arrests were out of the question ... after all, many of the officers, like Bubba, were also fans and they all enjoyed a good old fashioned bar brawl. Indeed, Enforcers and Fans alike saw it as a nice change from beating on the wife, the kids, the cat and the dog.

As they approached the exit, Percy sidled up to the Chief Enforcer.

As luck would have it, Percy knew the man. He was a regular, after hours client of Berty's Bingo Hall and Percy had in his possession some rather, shall we say, 'artistic' photos of that officer defying a more orthodox definition of what one, in this instance, might describe as 'nature'.

More damning still was the breach of that officer's limited club member's interaction status which the pictures revealed. It was no surprise therefore that the officer whole heartedly agreed to Percy's request for the Fan's identity cards to be inspected.

Of course, the only fan without a card was Moose.

CHAPTER THIRTEEN

Colonel Conga took the call as he sat eating dinner in the officer's canteen.

It was Percy. He was calling from the Tipsy Turd.

The Dobberman was overcome with excitement and nerves. Conga was the main man, you see, and Percy knew that to waste his precious time was an invitation for trouble.

At first, Percy's mutterings made little sense to Conga who idly toyed with the food on his plate ... poking and swivelling a knife into the eye socket of a grilled fish. As he listened, Conga imagined it was the tiresome Dobberman on the plate and his eye socket under the knife.

At least that was until he deciphered a few of Percy's words and understood their significance ...

'Kingfish's accomplice ... apprehended ... on his way to you ... now!'

Conga jumped up with excitement. He knocked over a glass of milk which toppled off the table and spilt down his trousers. The stain looked like an embarrassing accident. In fact it disguised an embarrassing accident. Conga neither noticed nor cared. He bolted out of the canteen and down the stairs to the back entrance of the Central Enforcement Headquarters.

And there he waited, in eager anticipation, for the arrival, in the back of an armoured wagon, of one half of Morningtaria's most notorious, albeit only, crime syndicate.

CHAPTER FOURTEEN

'Get off me you fat lump!'

Bernice Kingfish swung her chubby forearm up and off the pillow. It swung on the axis of her chubby elbow before slamming downwards across the back of her chubby husband's head.

Bubba woke with a start.

'Wotcha do that for you fat pig?!' he bellowed and at the same time pounced on her with a swiftness and agility made all the more extraordinary by the fact that Bubba looked about as swift and agile as a lard sandwich.

Bubba straddled his wife, took hold of her big nose between his thumb and forefinger and twisted.

'Get off! ... GET OFF!' Bernice squealed like the fat pig she was.

After a few seconds, Bubba relented and let go of Bernice's snout.

'You're still drunk Bubba. You stink of it!'

'No I'm not you fat pig!' countered Bubba ... and he wasn't ... despite the twelve pints of Lager he had swilled in the Tipsy Turd a few hours earlier.

'You were trying to strangle me in your sleep!'

'Was I?' enquired Bubba 'Well I wish you hadn't woke me ... 'cos maybe I could have made a proper job of it ... you FAT PIG!'

'Get off! ... GET OFF!' Bernice screamed. She twisted her substantial bulk and Bubba, who despite his soberness was nonetheless still a bit giddy, fell off her, off the bed and landed in a heap on the floor.

Bernice seized her chance, sprung up and jumped on him ... punching and kicking ... hammering into Bubba as he made his retreat towards the bedroom door. It slammed behind him, leaving Bubba sprawled out on the landing of their two bedroom terrace house.

There he composed himself, struggled unsteadily to his feet and made his way downstairs to the couch.

The next morning, over breakfast, the atmosphere was no more frosty than usual and when it came time to leave for work, Bubba grunted his usual farewell to Bernice, picked up the lard sandwich she had made for his lunch, walked out the front door and made his way along Bobo Street to the bus stop.

Work was a release for Bubba. He was an Enforcement Officer and his department head was Colonel Conga.

Bubba looked up to the Colonel ... had done since The Great War against the Sundowners seventeen years earlier when he had served as a cadet under Conga.

For his part, the Colonel counted Bubba as a faithful servant ... not someone to share a confidence with ... but like a favourite dog whose good nature you might reward with a choccy drop ... or whose skull you might crush if it bit you.

'Any news sir?'

Bubba addressed the Colonel who was seated in a leather recliner in front of a large bay window through which he could look out over the city skyline.

They were in the Colonel's office, located on the 25th floor of Central Enforcer Headquarters.

The Colonel did not like being questioned ... especially from an underling. However, he did not snap at Bubba because the man was enquiring about his adopted son ... Smokey Kingfish ... and he knew that Bubba just might be the key to locating Kingfish.

For the Colonel, it was just a little too much of a coincidence that Bubba had been drinking in the same bar, at the same time as the mysterious stranger they had apprehended the night before.

As was the Colonel's habit, he answered Bubba's query with one of his own.

'No Bubba ... how about you?'

Bubba ignored the question. He had come this far and had to speak his mind ... whatever the consequences.

'Since I've known you sir ... ever since Sundowner ... you've always been straight with me ... you let me keep Smokey. I know I snapped that day on the beach ... was sick of killing ... and I couldn't have blamed you if you'd shot me for treason. I disobeyed a direct order, sir. But I'd just killed his parents you see. When I found the poor lad hidden under that basket of fish, well ... I just couldn't do **that** ... sir. You risked your own commission, what with discharging me that day and letting me back to Morningtaria with Smokey ... even letting me and Bernice keep him. I know he's done a terrible thing sir but if ... when you find him, sir ... you won't hurt him, will you sir?'

Conga stood up. He walked over to Bubba, embraced him and patted him on the back. He kept patting ... for a good twenty seconds ... enjoying a little daytime fantasy ... of plunging a serated combat knife, time and time again, into Smokey Kingfish's back.

Eventually, the Colonel pulled away and looked Smokey's surrogate father in the eye.

'Of course I won't Bubba.'

CHAPTER FIFTEEN

Moose fell in and out of consciousness. He couldn't move ... a situation every bit to do with the drugs swimming around his blood as it had to the leather restraints attaching him to a chair. He didn't know where he was but that didn't much matter because he hadn't yet been able to ask himself that question.

He was, of course, in the interview room of Colonel Conga who at that moment was seated in darkness beside him, silently observing through night vision goggles, and recording everything Moose said, even though the words seemed only to form a delirious and incoherent mutter.

The Colonel had given Moose a 'Truth Treatment'.

Among other pioneering efforts in the field of Interrogation, Conga had developed the use of truth drugs and the liquid coursing into Moose's vein via a catheter attached to his left arm, was the Colonel's Secret Recipe, consisting of ten parts 'Dreamscape', a Scooberry derived hallucinogenic, to three parts 'Babble' an amphetamine developed for its tongue loosening qualities.

The Colonel trusted no one with the job of administering those drugs and he alone knew the correct doses and necessary procedures involved. Conga was loath to share them with anybody. He had a passion for conducting interrogations and by endeavouring always to be the sole purveyor of the most advanced techniques, Conga ensured every enforcer beat a path to his door when they had a suspect requiring 'special treatment'.

As the Colonel sat watching, Moose suddenly threw open his eyes and stared, unblinking, into the darkness.

If the room had been fully lit, Moose's view would have been no different for he was impervious to his surroundings.

Moose saw plenty but none of what was contained in the Interview Room.

****

Moose was drowning. He was deep ... getting deeper. Daylight danced on the surface above his head. It shimmered, before his fading sight, with images of the past and future.

He saw himself.

He was Surfing.

He followed his own image as it sped beneath a crystalline curl in the tube of an endless wave. Smooth and curved above him, it might have vanished in its own transparency but for the dark shadow that formed a path along its face. The path led to daylight. It was the fall line and the rail of Moose's surfboard cut a deep track upon it.

He saw beyond to the sunlight at the end of the tube. In the eye through which it shone, other images danced back and forth ... images of all that had been good in his life. Beautiful twins. A baby girl ... his infant sister Fanny wrapped tight in a silken robe and snuggled up with another ...

A blonde baby boy.

He saw Kipper ... dear clumsy old Kipper, tangled in his own fishing line, laughing heartily as he stumbled and fell flat on his back.

Finally, he saw a faded picture ... his mother and father, stood together on a distant shore ... waving goodbye.

All that was good drew further away as the eye grew smaller. Moose's image still rode fast and true, but the wave was rushing into a storm beach and the sand it drew turned the tube murky and Cavern-like. It amplified the swish of breaking water into the deep roar of beasts unleashed that chased him and clawed at the tail of his surfboard from the bubbling cauldron of foam in his wake.

Moose viewed himself from the front now. He saw his image and the beasts that chased him. They were the demons of his past. Their faces grotesque ... their bodies twisted into frenzied dance and abominable copulation. Moose saw their eyes ... great saucers of black focussed on his own ... they pierced his soul and released the lust, the mayhem and the murder that resided there.

The demons disappeared and he saw once again his drowning self. The struggle was over and his face shone with the tranquillity of one redeemed. But Moose turned away ... he turned and where the back of his head should have been, a second face appeared. It was still his face but the tranquillity was gone, his gentle smile replaced with a hyena's grin of madness and his eyes, by the dark saucers of the demons. Moose still recognised himself ... but now he saw evil. The head turned once again, to reveal the good face. Then again, to reveal the bad. It never turned back, but revolved, slowly at first, growing faster ... good face ... bad face ... good ... bad ... good ...bad ... goodness ... evil ... LOVE ... HATE. Moose looked on in horror. The head span faster and faster. He grew dizzy. He sank deeper and deeper ... into the dark ... pressure growing unbearable ... closing in ... deeper ... darker ... overcoming him ... then nothing.

Moose saw nothing. He felt nothing.

But then ... a light.

From a door opening. A silhouette entering a room ... Moose looking up but unable to get up. The silhouette leaning over him, looking at him then receding into a chair by his side. Then it was speaking, the voice of Skipper Kipper, so close but coming to him like a distant echo borne on a wind of uncertain direction.

'Good face ... bad face' began Kipper 'Love and hate. Two sides of the same coin ... two sides of you. My dear Moose, you encourage the one yet stifle and confound the other ... but it does not weaken. The other side is frustrated but is patient and grows stronger from the wait. Love or hate so denied, inevitably returns and the longer it has waited, the stronger, more forcible the return.

Together they are driving you Moose ... love and hate ... they drive your spirit ... two sides, the one reacting with the other ... two droplets of water on a smooth ocean, chasing each others' tail ... circular motion and forward momentum ... moving forward ... creating a wave.'

'But what if I want nothing to do with the bad in me?' asked Moose.

'Can I ever be rid of the evil?'

'You cannot cleanse your soul of the evil residing there' replied Kipper. 'To do so would serve only to slow its outward journey towards enlightenment. It is a simple truth, Moose, that what is good is only so because of the remainder which is bad. Just as the lights leading to safe harbour are bright because they are surrounded by the dark of night.'

'Must I encourage the evil with murder then?'

'Never!' countered the Skipper 'Evil may lead to murder, but rarely is it the other way round. Murder leads to remorse. Why feel bad for what you have done? Surely it is better to feel good for what you haven't? You see Moose, there is always a choice. With some, it is ignored and in other unfortunates it may never be considered, but it is, nonetheless, always there. Murder is an act borne of evil. Choosing to deny the act is noble, but it does not deny the evil itself. To do so would solve nothing. Do not stifle the evil Moose. Embrace it for it is a passion ... energy not to be squandered. It can be channelled; it is fuel for the imagination and can be turned to good. Evil is Hate, Moose. So hate with a passion what is evil!'

****

Conga left the interview room and without bothering to remove his night-vision goggles, walked to a small washroom across the hallway.

Once inside, he kept the light switched off. His goggles were heat sensitive and whilst relieving himself, it amused Conga to imagine his Willy as a Ray-Gun, strafing wrongdoers lined up against the urinal wall with a beam of luminous, killer pee.

Once finished, Conga holstered his rather insubstantial weapon, zipped his fly and returned to the interview room. He opened the door. Light from the hallway flooded in. It fell on the prisoner and his eyes flew open. The Colonel walked over to Moose, leant over the chair and examined him closely.

'What is your name?' asked Conga.

Moose nodded and his expression changed but he said nothing.

'WHAT IS YOUR NAME?' Conga repeated.

Expression changed to one more tranquil - but still no reply.

'Can you hear me?'

No response.

'Do you know where you are?'

Nothing.

'WHERE IS SMOKEY KINGFISH?'

Moose's expression darkened ... but that was all.

The Colonel was flummoxed. He had never before observed such strange behaviour. The prisoner who certainly was not aware of Conga's questions appeared to be consorting with some imaginary presence.

Conga sat down and wondered what his next course of action might be.

He had taken the truth treatment far beyond its usual limits and quite clearly, it was not having the desired effect.

'Should I get out the Tool Box?' he asked himself aloud.

'Perhaps it is too late' he pondered. 'Perhaps the 'Dreamscape' has caused irreparable damage in which case little will be gained from torturing a vegetable.'

'No' he concluded 'I must be patient. I must come up with a devious and brilliant plan. After all, am I not Conga ... a most devious and brilliant Muddlehead ?'

... And he was ... and true to his word, Conga came up with a plan and whilst it was not a particularly devious or brilliant one - relying simply on the prisoner regaining consciousness and leading him, unwittingly, to Smokey Kingfish - it was, on the whole, a pretty good effort for a Muddlehead.

****

And so, in accordance with the finer detail of his plan, that evening the Colonel had the unconscious Moose dumped in a deserted alley behind the Morningtarian Surf Beach ... and ordered Percy Snivel, the Dobberman, to keep watch.

****

True to the Colonel's wishes, sometime around midnight the following evening, Moose awoke and whilst he looked terrible, Snivel noted that he was lucid and despite the 'Dreamscape', appeared to be of this world and not, as the boss had feared, orbiting some distant planet inhabited by a herd of banjo playing pink elephants in lederhosen and smoking cheroots.

Moose himself had no recollection of his 'truth treatment' and perhaps more important, to Conga at least, did not suspect that he was being watched. Indeed, all Moose could recall from the last three days, was a wave, some demons and a thought provoking encounter with Skipper Kipper. His recollection of these things was crystal clear which was strange because he knew they had all been from a dream.

Despite having been asleep for so long, Moose was still very tired and decided the best thing to do would be to lie back down and get a bit more kip.

This did not please Percy Snivel.

The dobberman was already extremely cheesed off having been hidden, crouched uncomfortably inside a smelly garbage container, for over a day and a half now.

'Why won't that scuzzbucket Conga send someone to relieve me?' he grumbled.

It was all getting too much for the little weasel and with the prospect of being stuck for another few hours waiting for his target to wake up, Percy's willpower crumbled so that the moment he spied Moose was asleep, he sneaked out of the alley and headed to his favourite Bingo Hall.

For Percy, it was an unfortunate move made all the worse because his planned one hour's absence extended into five.

He had meant only to 'relieve' himself, returning to his post in less time than it takes to skin a chicken with a chainsaw ... but a lengthy and curious liaison between Percy, two fat ladies and the aforementioned chicken put paid to that.

By the time Percy Snivel returned to the alley ... Moose was gone.

****

Conga was furious, and it showed - in the terrified expression on Percy Snivel's face - a face frozen onto a head which moments earlier had been separated from its body and laid to rest on the bloody interview room floor. Conga kicked the head in frustration. 'Where could the prisoner be?' He swivelled and smashed his boot into Percy's nether regions causing a fountain of gunk to squirt from Percy's neck. 'Why didn't this fool stay in the alley when he was told?' Conga screamed before returning to his chair.

He sat down, closed his eyes and began to think.

Conga was smart. On the Muddlehead scale of things, he was positively brilliant. But the Kingfish Mystery, as he called it, had so far eluded him. Conga guessed that superiors and minions alike were following his progress, or lack thereof, watching closely, delighting in his setbacks and wallowing in every opportunity to ridicule him.

'Even that dimwit, Captain Longbone has the nerve to shoot his fat mouth off in the canteen about me loosing my touch,' the Colonel thought. But then he smiled to himself ... 'He'll pay for it though!'

It was a light-hearted thought and one which summed up the Colonel's general frame of mind, for despite the frustrations of the case, he was really quite enjoying himself. Conga felt stimulated not least because of the nasty fantasies which grew more vivid with every passing day. Images of what he would do to the elusive Smokey Kingfish ... despite the assurances he had given Bubba.

They swirled inside his head when he lay down at night ... casting him to sleep upon a sweet lullaby of screams as Smokey's teeth were extracted ... with an ice pick.

The fantasies were born of Conga's evil imagination ... one unique among the Muddleheads. Indeed, whilst there were plenty of bad people in Morningtaria, there were none with any kind of imagination half as lucid or as downright evil as the Colonel's. Why would they need one? When the Bosspigs had all the answers ... as well as all the questions. The average Muddlehead certainly didn't need an imagination to pick a fight with a rival Bongoball fan. Or to toss a sack filled with rocks and cats into the river.

To the Muddleheads ... those things came naturally.

Perhaps Conga's uniqueness came from a willingness to develop his exceptional imagination. The process went hand in hand with the exercise of his deductive powers ... so necessary when it came to crime-solving. Conga regarded these highly-tuned functions of his brain in much the same way he regarded the items in his tool box. They all assisted in the fulfilment of his evilness, which in this case was the sadistic and excruciating punishment he would inflict upon Smokey Kingfish ... given the chance.

It was the evil which drove the Colonel's imagination and as he sat pondering in the interview room, it was what caused him to arrive at the most simple but brilliant of deductions.

On the seat beside him ... the one so recently occupied by Moose, sat a cap ... a distinctive cap ... a Sailor's Cap.

'That's it!'

A spark of comprehension went off in the Colonel's head.

'All this began just metres from the ocean, in Turd Cove ... RIGHT NEXT DOOR TO THE HARBOUR!'

He thought of the many ships which used the harbour ... Morningtaria's largest. Had the prisoner, so recently misplaced by Percy Snivel, arrived on one of these vessels ? Had Smokey Kingfish made good his escape in one?

The Colonel jumped out of his chair, picked up the cap, rushed from the interview room and out of the building.

He marched down the street towards the harbour. It was less than half a mile from the Central Enforcement Headquarters.

The closer he got, the more Conga felt his spirits lift.

'At last!' he thought 'I have a lead!'

For the first time in quite a while, he felt confident ... Conga felt confident because he felt he knew what he might find at the harbour ... a cap less skipper with departure on his mind.

****

When he arrived some minutes later, Conga made his way to the Harbourmaster's Office located on the pier head.

With a flourish, he pushed open the door and breezed inside.

In front of him was a large open room. It was filled with a hotchpotch of dowdy old desks and swivel chairs; clunky typewriters and dusty spider plants.

Conga surveyed the scene.

The Harbour Office employees were busily beavering away ... taking care of Harbour Office business ... rustling important papers and sorting staples into their respective sizes.

Conga noticed how they all appeared to blend in to their surroundings.

An old man wearing a tie, braces and a green and blue cardigan shuffled up to Conga.

'Can I be of assistance sir?' he asked.

'Yes' replied Conga 'Take me to your Boss.'

'Yippee!' thought the old man recognising his chance to unwind a bit of red tape.

'Have you an appointment sir?' he countered.

At once, Conga produced his identity card and slapped it against the old man's forehead.

'TAKE ME NOW!' he screamed.

Unsurprisingly, Conga was immediately taken to the Harbourmaster.

He was led up an open flight of stairs and into a smaller, glass-faced room which overlooked the general office.

Inside, the Colonel was confronted by a rather small, owlish looking chap seated behind a desk upon which a carved wooden sign announced ... 'Gregorious Trout - Harbourmaster'.

'Trout' barked Conga without pausing to introduce himself. 'Have you seen this man?' and tossed before the speechless Harbourmaster a photograph taken of Moose on the evening of his capture.

A petrified Trout immediately picked up the photo and held it up to the light, no more than one nose length from the bottle-bottom spectacles he wore.

He stared hard.

The atmosphere grew tense.

Conga tapped his fingers on the desk.

A bead of sweat formed on Trout's forehead and rolled onto his nose.

His stomach rumbled.

Conga sighed and looked around impatiently.

Trout stared harder and then ... 'YES!' he exclaimed in a tone of orgasmic relief 'I recognise him! It's Moose from off the SS Bulldog' and with a quivering stab of his forefinger pointed out the window towards a rusting old freighter tied up across the way.

'That's her, moored over yonder' Trout concluded before sinking back, exhausted into his chair.

Gregorious Trout's office, Conga considered as he gazed in the direction of the SS Bulldog, offered an ideal position from which to spy the comings and goings from that vessel.

He stood silent for a minute, staring out the window, scheming his next move.

And all the while, Gregorious sat, not daring to speak, his legs shaking beneath his desk.

The silence was almost unbearable for old Trout, a nervous fellow at the best of times and when the Colonel turned and fixed a predatory stare in his direction he did not know where to look.

Slowly, the feared Enforcer walked from the window and around the desk until he stood directly behind Trout.

When, after an awfully long pause, Trout felt Conga's hands on his shoulders, he half expected it to be the last thing he might ever feel.

Instead, the hands pulled him backwards so that Trout's chair rolled out from under the desk on its coasters. Finally, Trout was dragged across the office and out the door.

Without so much as a word, Conga had commandeered Trout's office and left the poor Harbourmaster frozen in his chair at the top of the stairs ... gibbering and peeing into his pants as the full complement of his staff gaped from the office below.

CHAPTER SIXTEEN

Early in the morning, Moose weighed anchor and steered the SS Bulldog out to sea.

The Colonel's wait was over.

In the three days since his arrival, Conga had remained almost continuously inside Gregorious Trout's office, a surveillance camera glued to his face and trained on the SS Bulldog.

His only concern during that time was the possibility someone might let slip to Moose that he was under surveillance. Nobody therefore had been allowed into Trout's Office ... in case they noticed the direction Conga's camera was pointed.

In hindsight, such a measure was a little paranoid on the Colonel's part, seeing as the likelihood of Trout's staff venturing up those stairs, was remote to say the least.

They were, after all, Civilservs, a rather timid bunch who never did anything quite as rebellious as something they had not been asked to do in the first place.

Nevertheless, Conga was not inclined to take a chance, so they were barred.

... With the exception of Gregorious Trout.

He was allowed into his own office ... not as a conciliatory gesture on the Colonel's part. Far from it! Conga had demoted the poor old sausage to sandwich and tea fetching duties.

How humiliating! Trout was absolutely gutted ... and what made things worse was the method by which he was summoned.

Gregorious, you see, had a ceremonial scarlet rope dangling from the ceiling in his office. It ended in an intricate and beautifully plaid bobble which hung just above his desk.

Gregorious enjoyed his life as Harbourmaster and whilst he took to all his tasks with gusto, by far the most pleasurable was the periodic tug he was obliged to give that rope. Why was it so thrilling? Well, the rope led to a big brass bell mounted in a tower on the roof. Whenever

Trout tugged, the bell rang, thus signalling to his staff, the Docksters and all interested parties, the arrival of a ship into port.

Trout loved tugging on his rope. Loved the rich resonating 'bong' of his bell ... loved the sound of hastened activity it induced in his staff ... loved the sense of power.

But what he did not love was somebody tugging his rope for him.

... And Conga tugged all day long.

How very confusing it was for those persons whose daily lives were dictated by the arrival and departure of ships. Why did they hear the bell at intervals disparate to all maritime movement?

Gregorious knew why.

Whereas before, the ringing had sent delightful tingles up his spine, now it sent a cold shiver. It meant he had to enter that room again ... to present himself to that frightful beast ... to make more sandwiches and brew more tea.

****

The Colonel sipped on his cuppa and watched as the SS Bulldog made its way through the pier heads and out to sea.

He was happy because everything was going to plan.

Conga had observed Moose on several occasions during the last three days and had learnt much more about his movements from an extremely reluctant but nonetheless reliable source. The Mechanics.

Whilst in port, the SS Bulldog had undergone a number of minor engine repairs and Moose had employed the Mechanics to carry them out.

Later, inevitably, they had been apprehended by the Colonel under the false pretext of a random tool inspection.

As a Club, the Mechanics were proud to be called Tradesmen and practised their craft to the exclusion of all others, secure in the knowledge their specific skills were protected not only by the rigid demarcation set down by the Bosspig controlled unions but by the law itself.

In Morningtaria, if a Carpenter was caught with say, a wrench, whilst he might avoid a head explosion, he most certainly would not avoid the wrath of the Mechanics. It was the same for all trades. Indeed, that very week, the local newspaper, The Bosspig Bugle, had reported on an unfortunate incident involving the Plumbers and how it had come to their attention that a Bricklayer by the name of Bartholomew Cockroach had been found with a U Bend in his possession. Later, the Plumbers had acted entirely within the law by employing that same U Bend as a conduit through which to insert three metres of barbed wire into Cockroach's intestine via the only 'O' ring a bricklayer could legitimately (or anatomically) carry on his person.

With the story of the unfortunate Cockroach scuttling inside their minds, it was little surprise the Mechanics agreed to spy for Conga, especially when he 'conjured' a brush from one of their tool bags and threatened to tell the Painters!

****

Whilst the intelligence the Mechanics gathered was hardly intelligent, it proved nonetheless very useful to the Colonel who found out the very day the SS Bulldog was due to set sail.

What he failed to learn, however, was the ship's intended destination.

Moose, it seems had been extremely vague, only submitting his departure date to the Mechanics in the hope they might speed up and finish their work on time ... and although they had sat with him on several occasions during tea breaks, the Mechanics had ultimately been unsuccessful in steering the conversation onto a course whereby Moose divulged that destination.

What's more, the Colonel, even with his considerable resources, was unable to employ more official means to find out. That was because in Morningtaria a Captain was not obliged to inform the authorities of where his ship was headed or even what cargo she carried.

Conga could hardly complain though. Such laxity, after all, was for his benefit as well as all the other Bosspigs and Chief Enforcers who supplemented their already huge incomes via a myriad of secretive and highly lucrative smuggling operations ... importing illicit goods, which they themselves had banned, in order to make more by selling them on the black-market.

For once then, Conga was let down by the State.

Did he mind?

Not on your Nelly!

Conga was not the least concerned because, as it turns out, he had decided to follow the SS Bulldog … in his father's sailing boat!

****

Chief Bertie Bosspig, the President of Morningtaria was, as coincidence would have it, Conga's old man. Of course, he was extremely wealthy and quite naturally enjoyed those expensive leisure activities reserved in Morningtaria for the Bosspigs.

None more so than sailing.

Indeed, Bertie was the proud owner of a fifteen metre Offshore Racing Catamaran which he had named after Primrose, his favourite, although sadly departed mistress. (She had committed suicide on her thirtieth birthday by shooting herself in the back of the head … five times.)

Primrose was surely the most beautiful sailing vessel in all of Morningtaria. Her design, a triumph of Berty's own doing, pandered not to creature comfort, but speed.

Sitting on her mooring, she shone brilliant white … sleek lines dazzling beneath unblemished bright work … ready to let loose onto open sea … to soar and swoop amidst the waves.

Conga, whilst appreciating the aesthetics of Primrose, rarely got to sail her. These days, he did not care for recreational pursuit. In his youth though, Conga had been an avid sailor. He had learnt the ropes, so to speak and whilst in later years, those ropes had no longer been attached to sails but to the necks of wrongdoers, be it conviction, or the over confidence of a buffoon, Conga still felt to sail Primrose was well within his capabilities.

More important, he felt his father would feel the same way.

'Daddy always told me how good I was at sports.' he concluded to himself.

And it was true.

Bertie always had.

... And that was why, after despairing for so long over his son's reluctance to pursue the sporting life, when asked to borrow the Primrose, he had jumped for joy.

'Dear boy!' Bertie had cried as he sat with his son in the smoking room of the Royal Empirical Colonic and Republican Yacht Club.

'Surely you indulge me ... are you rejoining us Bosspigs ? Have you at last resigned yourself to a noble life of leisure?'

Conga, who from an early age had quite systematically and deviously earned himself a plum position amongst his siblings as the apple of his father's eye ... evaded the question.

****

And so it was, with his tea in his tum and the SS Bulldog steaming towards the horizon, Conga got up, sauntered out of the Harbourmaster's office and made his way to the Yacht Marina, where he found Primrose primed and ready to set sail.

The Colonel climbed aboard and with the minimum of fuss, fired up the outboard motors, cast off and 'put-putted' out to sea.

Some minutes later, having stowed the mooring lines and fenders, Conga returned to the helm, set his course, leant back against the binnacle and took stock.

Primrose was designed for single-handed sailing. Her rigging was simple and both the Mainsail and Jib could be trimmed from the safety of the cockpit. Additionally, the steering was taken care of by a sophisticated auto helm which enabled Conga to maintain a constant course whilst attending to other duties.

All in all, he was in pretty good shape.

Primrose virtually sailed herself and that would give Conga time to keep track of the SS Bulldog ... a task which he suspected might prove tricky.

The Colonel had not been in such a hurry to leave directly after the SS Bulldog. He was concerned that he should stay out of sight beyond the horizon. In this regard he felt able to maintain such a discreet distance because of a homing device covertly attached to the SS Bulldog's hull by the Mechanics. It enabled him to keep track of the ship from up to twenty nautical miles away ... a distance within which, Conga was confident, the ultra-fast Primrose could remain.

"We shall see." Conga speculated as he watched the SS Bulldog shrink to a speck on the Northern horizon.

CHAPTER SEVENTEEN

Even though Colonel Conga was a clever man, he was unable to be in two places at the same time. During his three day occupation of Gregorious Trout's office he had been entirely absent from the Headquarters of the Chief Enforcers. Indeed, the only time he had left the Harbourmaster's Office was to visit his father and subsequently to attend to the provisioning of Primrose.

Everybody at Headquarters had wondered where he was. It was after all, most unlike the Colonel not to turn up for work.

Everybody had wondered but not one of the Enforcers had taken steps to find out. They knew better than to meddle in the affairs of the Boss.

All that was, except one.

That man knew where the Colonel was. He had known all along because he had followed Conga to the harbour and had stayed there ever since, watching Conga's every movement.

What a foolhardy thing to do but there again, that man was rather stupid. More importantly though, he was spurred on by a mission, and the motivation alone fuelled his brain with just enough juice to energise itself into producing a mind blowing deduction ...

'The Boss is goin somewhere on that boat he's filling with grub.'

And on the strength of that deduction, the man made a life changing decision.

Big ol' Bubba smuggled himself onboard the Primrose.

****

Seeing as Bubba was such a large dough boy, it is hard to imagine how the Colonel, once he had set sail, did not detect the presence of another body onboard.

The indications were there. Primrose was more than a little unbalanced.

The cause ... Bubba's substantial arse, which had wedged itself inside the anchor locker in the starboard bow. Unfortunately for Conga, instead of considering that Primrose's ungainliness was due to something simple ... like a 120 kilogram tub of lard stowed in the boat's furthest extremity ... he posted the blame squarely on the rigging, thus condemning himself to spend a disproportionate amount of the next few days tinkering and meddling with sheets, halyards, lanyards, winches, vangs and lazy jacks in a futile attempt to rectify what was, in reality, an irrelevant blemish in the overall abomination that was his own helmsmanship.

It added to an already exhausting passage.

For four whole days, the prevailing winds, screaming at gale force down the coast of Morningtaria, came from the North ... the same direction the SS Bulldog was headed.

She was steaming straight into the wind and this presented Conga with a problem.

Primrose's fastest point of sail, some forty five degrees off the wind, meant that every couple of hours, Conga was forced to tack from a North-westerly to a North-easterly heading and an hour after that, back again. Of course, all this zigzagging meant Primrose's 'distance made good' grew far less than the distance she was actually travelling over the water and so to keep up with the SS Bulldog, Conga had no other option than to sail Primrose at a far greater speed ... twenty knots to be exact ... a tremendous proposition.

Even so, Primrose was a thoroughbred and she managed to sustain the breakneck pace.

It helped that she was a racing catamaran and of a design which takes advantage of a phenomenon which allows such craft to sail faster into the wind than away from it.

Imagine, for example, a sprinter with the wind behind him. If he manages to run faster than the wind, he overtakes it and feels it in his face. Now just imagine if the wind in his face makes him go faster still. A chain reaction. The faster he runs ... the stronger the wind in his face ... and so the faster still he runs!

This is what was happening to Primrose. She was bringing the wind forward and strengthening it in relation to herself.

It is strange indeed to think that a breeze in the face can cause one to go faster than a breeze up one's chuff ... but for Primrose, this was true ... and whilst it augured well for Conga's aspirations to keep up with the SS Bulldog, the phenomenon had one serious downside ... a potentially catastrophic downside at that ... which the Colonel chose to ignore.

What if the chain reaction could not be controlled ?

What if, in the face of a strengthening wind, the sails could not be lowered or the boat steered away?

These are the circumstances an experienced sailor legislates against by keeping vigilant watch and ensuring the amount of sail aloft is no more than manageable.

But not Conga.

To sail at such a lightning pace, the foolhardy Colonel raised every square inch of canvas that was available to him ... and powered relentlessly onwards ... bashing to windward against a stiff breeze and confused swell.

It was horrific.

Whilst Primrose's bridge deck, which separated her two hulls, sat high above the water, the Colonel's reckless pace caused wave upon wave to pile-drive into it with a bone-jarring force.

It made things exceedingly uncomfortable for the Colonel but that was nothing to the discomfort felt by a scrunched up Bubba ... an agony of discomfort which in turn was nothing when compared to the horrendous strain placed on the boat herself.

How Primrose didn't buckle under the onslaught was testament only to Chief Bertie Bosspig's engineering prowess. It certainly was no thanks to the subtlety of Conga's seamanship. He chose to ignore the creaks and the moans emanating from Primrose's every edifice. He chose to ignore them because he chose to ignore the same strains emanating from his own sore and sleep deprived carcass. It was childish, but if he had to endure such discomfort, he sure was going to pass it on, with interest, to the 'stupid tub' beneath his feet.

The Primrose was no substitute for the victims of his Interview Room but abusing her this way sure made the Colonel feel better.

****

On his fourth night at sea, the wind died and Conga was forced to lower the outboard motors. At full throttle, they could only push the catamaran along at a miserly six knots. That was less than half the SS Bulldog's speed and by the morning, the tracking device had fallen silent.

No matter. By now, the Colonel had a pretty good idea where Moose was headed. The SS Bulldog hadn't once strayed from her Northerly course and as time wore on, it became clear that such a course could only lead to one destination - Moonshine.

At first light on the sixth day, Conga saw a Volcano - its dark outline towering above a thick bank of fog which clung to a far off coast.

The Colonel's thoughts turned to Moose. If he was right, and Moonshine was Moose's destination, then the tracking device would reactivate at any time and sure enough, as the sun broke free of the eastern horizon, Conga heard an unmistakable and reassuring 'beep-beep'.

He felt ecstatic.

By way of congratulation, Conga went below for a nice cup of tea.

Five minutes later, the Colonel, mug in hand, sat back contented in his chair. Everything had gone according to plan. He had overcome the foulest of weather; not to mention the intolerable quirkiness of Primrose (not once did he concede that Primrose had survived the voyage in spite of him); and best of all, surely he had uncovered the secret lair of his greatest adversary - Smokey Kingfish.

'YIPPEEEEE!!!' he cheered to himself.

****

Although Moonshine was visible on the horizon, the island was still several hours motoring away. Before tea, the Colonel had plotted his position twenty five nautical miles off the coast and calculated the time to his arrival at just over four hours.

With this in mind, Conga decided he might as well catch up on a well deserved kip. 'About time' he reasoned. After all, he hadn't slept the entire passage - a combination of adrenaline and caffeine sustaining him at the helm.

Conga put down his mug, set his alarm, settled back and in no time at all was fast asleep.

CHAPTER EIGHTEEN

At precisely the same time as Colonel Conga was nodding off, just nineteen nautical miles to the North of Primrose, the SS Bulldog came to rest in a small, sheltered cove on the South coast of Moonshine. On board, Moose made his way to the bow from where he dropped the anchor.

Once satisfied the ship was secure, he jumped overboard and swam from the SS Bulldog to a point on the adjacent shoreline where a shipping container sat beneath a nosy palm tree.

Moose barely gave the incongruous metal hulk a glance before bounding off along the beach.

He was intent on making it back to Look-at-Me Lagoon - via the western coastline - before nightfall.

At once though, Moose stubbed his toe on a nasty shard of coconut husk buried in the sand ... and whilst it didn't so much as bleed, on the other side of the island, his sister simultaneously reached down beneath her sheets to scratch a curious little itch on her own toe.

****

Fanny, thus awoken and comprehending through drowsy eyes that the sun was already risen, climbed out of bed.

She was alone on the fishing platform.

Her usual companions, Smokey and Kipper, had set off in a small outrigger the previous evening to go deep sea fishing. They had not bothered to invite her which at the time had been upsetting and now, the next morning, infuriating.

'MEN!' she meeped out loud, at once invoking an image of Smokey and Kipper in her own ritualistic idea of what 'male-bonding' supposedly was all about ... of two men, nay deserters, who should have known better, sitting opposite each other in a boat, taking turns at swearing, burping and farting.

It was a funny image and without realising, Fanny no longer felt miffed ... but light hearted, and in no time at all, her thoughts reverted to the day ahead.

She decided to spend it picking Scooberries, a leisurely morning's consolation, luxuriating in the warm sun, munching her way through a dozen or so of those delicious fruits. Afterwards, she might collect the leftover pits in her basket and present them to naughty old Kipper for his next batch of Zappo. She rather hoped this might cause the old sausage to squirm and blush with the embarrassment of one receiving a gift from one he loves, but one, nonetheless, he has neglected to take fishing!

Fanny climbed down from the fishing platform and waded ashore.

She stopped on the beach ... observing the morning.

She loved this time. How tranquil it was ... everything silent ... in awe of its own beauty and demanding of its inhabitants pause before commencement of the day's business.

After some minutes, Fanny moved off the beach and began her journey inland through the mangrove swamp towards the lower slopes of the Volcano where the Scooberry patch lay.

She hurried along.

The swamp was a damp, forbidding place and as she negotiated her way through its rotting vegetation, Fanny began to feel ill at ease.

It was foul smelling at the best of times, but today, a stronger odour similar to that which often discharged itself from Kipper's bottom, overwhelmed the place.

Keen to leave the stench behind, Fanny broke into a run and whilst the terrain was not ideally suited to sprinting, she somehow managed it, punching her knees into the air and forging a path through the swamp until it gave way to open ground.

Fanny stopped to catch her breath.

Once the pounding of her heart subsided, more subtle bodily sensations began to make their way to Fanny's brain. Her legs felt itchy where they had been submerged in the putrid swamp water and upon looking down, Fanny was mildly distressed to find them covered in an angry red rash.

Bravely though, she shrugged it off and continued on her way.

A half hour later, Fanny arrived at the Scooberry patch.

She set down her basket and rested by a spring around which the bright green Scooberry bushes grew. During dry season, the spring was a valuable source of drinking water - crystal clear, cool and refreshing. Now though, Fanny was shocked to see steam rising up in ghostly wisps from the dirty, brackish water.

Curious, she could not resist the urge to dip her big toe into the water.

Such a silly thing to do.

The water was scalding hot and although she extricated her pinkie almost instantly, Fanny was not quick enough to avoid an excruciating burn.

She hopped over to the long grass. It was the special place where she and Smokey had first made love. There, Fanny lay down and let the tears well into her eyes.

'What's happening?!' she sobbed aloud 'Why are you picking on me?' she asked of her island home 'Snot fair!' she concluded.

It was all too much ... and the unanswered questions coupled with her physical pain caused Fanny to bawl her tender little heart out.

****

Fanny lay on the grass, staring into space. Her crying ceased ... self pity gone ... replaced by a memory. Of last night ... a conversation with Kipper. The real reason, she confessed, for her upset.

Kipper had taken her to one side.

'My darling Fanny' he had begun 'Do not be too sad or too mad at the mutterings of an old man. I do not mean to hurt you with the things I am to say ... but they are true and shortly will be revealed to you.'

Fanny was used to the rambling, roundabout way the Skipper meandered through a sentence. It was all so much gumph but gumph, nonetheless, enjoyable to Fanny coming as it did from such a kind old dumpling.

Kipper had continued...

'Firstly, it is love which fills your heart. You are all good and whilst my affection for you knows no bounds, it is not why I say this thing. I say it not as well-intentioned but idle compliment ... but as truth ... for truth is what it is and to know yourself ... it is what you must know.'

He moved closer ... close enough to whisper out of range of Smokey Kingfish who was seated, fiddling with a length of twine, on the far side of the fishing platform.

'A second truth concerns Smokey.'

The name uttered from the Skipper's lips was spoken softly but caught Fanny's attention just as sharply as if screamed through a megaphone.

'Circumstance will keep you apart.'

'WHAT DOES HE KNOW?' she thought.

'His path is different to yours ... but do not worry ... your soul mate is not Smokey but another whom you will meet with shortly ... and will know to be so ... for he will make you complete.'

Fanny pulled away. She was shocked. She loved the Skipper deeply but the moment made her realise her love for Smokey was deeper.

Kipper moved with her. He placed a gentle hand on her shoulder and coaxed Fanny to sit again.

'Try not to feel sad' he said 'The future is not bleak. You and Smokey may not be together but you will be fulfilled. Without each other your lives will be complete.'

Kipper paused. He left Fanny to ponder on his words before continuing.

'Finally' he resumed 'I have a third truth. It concerns us all ... you, me, Smokey and Moose. It is to do with Moonshine. Our time in this place is nearly at an end. Soon, all of us will move on.

'Where will we go?' asked Fanny.

The Skipper rose from his seat. He had started to cry and not wishing to upset Fanny, masked his tears with a head hung low. He moved to the edge of the fishing platform where, a minute earlier, Smokey had been. Now, the youth sat waiting for him in the outrigger. Finally, as Kipper climbed down, he answered.

'My dear' he concluded 'We must each go our separate ways.'

****

The clouds above her changed and changed again. From dog to duck to puffed up shadow cast face. She stared through them unregistering. Her sight instead ... inward looking ... seeing images not of pictures but of words ... Kipper's.

Fanny had been in the Scooberry patch for over an hour and still she pondered over what the Skipper had said to her the night before.

During her short life, she had learnt much from him.

She had learnt about human beings - their nature and circumstance.

The Skipper knew of such things ... knew of the human soul. He knew of the spirit's eternal journey ... how it followed every other spirit before it and how those spirits were the guardians of every feeling, thought and experience ... the guardians of all history.

History, carried forth on an endless procession of waves ... fanning outwards - out and away from the turbulent earth. Those waves - that history - all a part of Watersplash, sustaining his journey into the nothingness which encircled everything.

Fanny had learnt of duality.

'That which is bad is only so because of the remainder ... which is good.'

'Love and hate' the Skipper had preached 'Two drops of saltwater on a smooth ocean.'

'Love and hate. Therein lies the key ... unholy alliance ... for they are bound by each other. Goodness and evil, chasing one another's tail ... circular motion ... creating forward momentum ... creating a wave.'

'And they must be set free ... love and hate.'

'They drive imagination and unshackled will rise up to smash through barricades of ignorance. Duality that grows strong. Darkness and light becoming more so ... undiluted contrast neither blend nor shade but a pureness ... utter good ... utter evil ... appalled by each other ... until such emotion stirs imagination ... generator of untainted knowledge and, eventually, history ... which is conceived then carried hence atop a messenger ... a wave ... smoother of the way ... whose name is Watersplash.'

Fanny, in the Scooberry patch, applied the Skipper's rambling to herself.

'You are all good' had been his first truth.

She interpreted this to mean she lacked duality.

It led her to the second truth and why Smokey was not for her.

'He will bring me nothing but love.'

'But that is not what I need ... more love? No ... my spirit will falter ... its journey frustrated ... **stuck within a reflection of itself.**'

'What I need is evil ... someone evil.'

It tied in to the Skipper's words ... 'This man you will meet with shortly, and will know him to be so.'

Then she wondered about Kipper's teaching and if somehow it related to herself and Smokey's more distant future.

He had told of a spirit's journey ... outward from the earth into eternity. How the wave that it was might one day come back.

'Return, just as I have ... a backwash ... carrying the teachings of pure knowledge to those placed best to embrace it.'

Fanny knew her own spirit was not destined for such things. Unlike the Skipper, she had no gift for unhindered, unearthly thought. But that, she learnt, didn't mean her own spirit would be lost. It too might be carried back. Returning ... not as messenger, not like the Skipper, but passively ... as the remembrance of a life once led ... two lives even ... a soul shared ... but returned as a Watersplash. Returned to help smooth the way for those who follow.

But what of Smokey?

He was a Muddlehead ... a child born of grey parents to a grey life.

Or so she thought.

'Did that matter?'

Fanny guessed not, for despite his dull background, Kipper had taken an interest in Smokey from the start ... had seen in him a simple but precious potential to imagine.

It was all that was needed

Surely then, this was why she and Smokey could never by right for each other. She wasn't but Smokey was, in the eyes of the Skipper at least ... complete.

In Smokey ... duality existed.

Fanny's head hurt. All those thoughts flashing through it made her dizzy but still she agonised over the Skipper's words, arriving lastly at the third truth.

'Our time in this place is nearly at an end.'

He had spoken of Moonshine.

'Might ...' Fanny wondered '... it have anything to do with me?'

Had she upset Moonshine? The rash on her legs ... the scalded toes?

Was Moonshine sending her a message?

'Is the island picking on me?'

Or worse, she thought.

'Does it want us out of here?'

Moonshine, of course, didn't give two cahoots about Fanny or the others.

It was an island, after all. And islands are large lumps of earth, sand and stone which do not hold grudges and certainly do not care about anyone or anything.

But Fanny wasn't so sure. Maybe loving Smokey atop the hallowed soil of Moonshine had proved disrespectful. Mother Earth, after all, might not have appreciated the pummelling given to her by Fanny's thrusting white buttocks.

'Was that the reason?'

'Was Mother Earth to blame then? ... The Bitter Old Sow!'

Fanny decided to find out ... and what better way than to ask the Skipper.

Without delay, and forgetting to gather up her basket, she jumped up and bounded off towards the lagoon.

Scooberry picking ... the original purpose of Fanny's inland excursion, had entirely been forgotten.

CHAPTER NINETEEN

Moose was a third of the way back to Look-at-me Lagoon.

The journey thus far, along the exposed windward coast of Moonshine had proved exhausting, what with the climbing required to overcome the dozen or so limestone points blocking the way.

Even the beaches made for difficult terrain, strewn as they were with the flotsam of a thousand storms ... all of which had to be scrambled over.

What a contrast from the tranquil, uncluttered lagoon to the North.

Here, there was no barrier reef to offer shelter from a malevolent ocean ... just a treacherous shore ... not safe for man or boat.

It was 9.30am.

Already, the sea-breeze had kicked in for the day ... whipping the ocean into a foam frenzy.

Moose sat for a minute on the rotting carcass of a storm-felled palm tree and surveyed the ocean.

His gaze fell upon the waves ... eyes drawing lines across the mountains of water forming in front of the beach. Those lines ... the tracks made by a surfboard upon which his imagination rode.

... And then something else.

Amidst the turmoil of whitecaps beyond the surf-line, Moose saw a larger, more solid shape.

He jogged to the end of the beach and climbed on top of a rocky outcrop. His elevated position gave Moose a better view and he was able to make out, perhaps a mile away, the distinctive white hulls of an upturned Catamaran.

CHAPTER TWENTY

Colonel Conga woke at 9.00am ...

... A violent transition from dream to nightmare ... from cosy bunk to cold cabin floor.

Primrose's motion ... fast and violent, had thrown him out of bed and the high-pitched scream of the Wind Generator signalled to Conga that the wind had increased to at least forty knots.

Although it wasn't in his nature to admit it, the Colonel knew he had made a serious mistake. He should have reefed the sails before going to sleep. Instead, both the main and the foresail remained fully extended to the top of the mast ... set to squeeze maximum energy from a minimal wind.

As he emerged from his cabin, the seriousness of his predicament became crystal clear.

Not only was the wind howling ... but howling in the face of Primrose, a headwind made all the stronger by the boats own momentum ... which built with every passing second ...

... And seconds were vital.

Conga had to act fast ... had somehow to slow the Catamaran down!

He quickly considered his options.

Could he turn Primrose away from the wind?

Too dangerous ... half way through such a manoeuvre and the sails would fill, causing the windward hull to lift and Primrose to flip over.

No ... the only chance was to ease the rigging and haul down the mainsail.

He clambered over to where the sheets were secured. One was attached to the boom via a complex system of pulleys attached to a traveller running the width of the bridge-deck. If Conga could only ease it, then the pulleys would slide to the leeward side, thus loosening the mainsail and dumping the wind.

At once, Conga twisted the sheet from its cleat and with a swift jerk, set it loose.

Unfortunately, the unwary Colonel failed to realise the tension in the mainsail was far too much for him to hold and his hand was pulled at a breakneck pace into the first of the pulleys.

'ARGGGGHHHH!'

... was his response ... perfectly reasonable under the circumstances.

Indeed, the circumstances were that the pulley could only accommodate rope one inch in diameter whereas the thickness of Conga's thumb and forefingers ... was two.

Clearly, the excess girth had to go ... and this was achieved in much the same way as reducing the excess girth of a banana by peeling it.

'ARGGGGHHHH!'

... The Colonel screamed again, as he watched the flesh from those digits roll back from the bones upon which, just seconds earlier, they had been attached.

The pain was horrific ... but the Colonel blocked it out.

He had to focus ... had to think.

All the while his thumb and forefingers were jammed, so to was the sheet in its pulley causing the mainsail to stay put and Primrose to go faster and further upwind.

'How the bloody hell do I get my hand free?'

Conga pulled on his thumb. He pulled with every bit of strength he had ... all the while fighting a tremendous urge to pass-out.

He had to get free ... had to slow Primrose down.

By now, she was travelling at a breakneck pace. Flying from wave to wave. One second, weightless, catapulted from a crest ... the next ... diving into a trough.

Conga continued his struggle whilst all around him was chaos ... a chaos of many components and all of his own making.

It is true to say that the maintenance of tidy decks had been a task wholly ignored by Conga during the voyage, and the price for his slovenly, unseamanlike conduct became apparent as any discarded item not fastened tight was picked up by the sheets of water slashing across the deck and hurled overboard.

A passing bucket caught Conga square in the face.

'Aaaarghhh!' he screamed before continuing the struggle with his thumb.

Finally ... a forward hatch ripped from its hinges ... smashed into the underside of the boom and deflected into Conga's groin.

'Ooooooooh!' he gasped.

It was the last straw.

Beaten ... Conga shrunk down and waited for the inevitable.

CHAPTER TWENTY ONE

Skipper Kipper was babbling.

'The spirit sheds lives as if casting aside old clothes.' he explained to Smokey as they sat fishing from the outrigger.

Smokey nodded attentively in the Skipper's direction but his thoughts were with the fish.

Kipper went on.

'And yours has shed many to get this far.'

'Indeed' he added ... 'every soul undertakes a journey ... an eternal journey ... and yours has travelled further along than most ... carried forth on a powerful wave ... progressing from previous lives unhindered by the excess baggage of past experience.'

'Smokey ... yours is an old soul ...'

The lad looked up. 'Sole?' he thought ... 'a tasty fish is Sole.'

'... it has gained a wealth of knowledge ... Noodlestones of experience ... and best of all ... has taught you to imagine ... to think pure thought.'

Kipper continued 'Smokey, for most, thought is conditioned by instinct ... a pre-requisite for idea and action. Refined over generations, instinct is potent and compels one to journey through life as if through a tunnel ... certain of one's direction only because no other choice is offered. Can a Lemming not fail to leap when reaching a cliff?'

'I wonder if Lemming tastes like Sole?' thought Smokey.

'But you Smokey ... your ideas stem from free will ... not need. Through a lack of conditioning, your soul has reached the highest state of one still subject to human restraint ... and soon it will discard human life altogether ... become fluid ... omnipotent ... passing on the purest of knowledge ... remembrance untainted to the souls that follow.'

... And all that Kipper explained was acknowledged by Smokey ...

... But not understood till much later.

In the meantime, Smokey's abrupt 'Yeah right' signalled to the Skipper it was time to shut his trap ... time to let the boy fish in peace.

****

The new dawn brought with it a substantial catch.

Smokey snagged a Yellow-fin Tuna. It was large enough for lunch ... and the last catch of the day, the duo deciding there was no need for more.

Because Kipper was rather lazy, he left the job of stowing the fishing gear to Smokey who, supposing this had much to do with the bearded bloater's advancing years, did not mind. In fact, it gave him immense pleasure to assist Kipper in every little way.

He felt it was the least he could do.

The Skipper leant back. He stretched out before the new sun's warming rays and with the contentment of one satisfied with the day's catch, closed his eyes and went to sleep.

At the same time, Smokey set about preparing to gut and fillet the Tuna.

It was women's work but even so, Smokey was inspired to present the Tuna 'oven-ready' ... to let Fanny marvel at his thoughtfulness.

'After all' he concluded 'What a fine example of sexual equality!' ... which incidentally was a new idea, having found its genesis, just a few days earlier, in Smokey's head no less!

****

Skipper Kipper woke at 9.45am.

Smokey had forgotten about the Tuna and instead was busying himself with the outrigger's rigging, trimming it against the growing wind and sea.

'Shall we be heading back?' he asked just a little concerned.

'Not just yet' replied Kipper 'I fancy a dip ... back in a while!'

... And just like that, the furry old codger slipped over the side and swam away.

CHAPTER TWENTY TWO

Colonel Conga found himself approximately twenty five feet above sea-level.

He was in mid-air ... catapulted from a 'pitch-polled' catamaran.

How quickly it had happened.

One second, Primrose had soared atop a crest, the second, she had plummeted beneath the next ... which stood vertical, preventing the hapless craft from ever again pointing skyward.

Primrose had pierced the water ... forward momentum lost ... and from the stern, her hulls had thrust skyward, overtaking the bows with such a velocity, the Colonel was projected out of the cockpit.

Before splashing down, a number of thoughts passed through the Colonel's mind. Indeed, as he flew through the air, it was surprising just how much he managed to think. He resigned himself to a salty sea-grave and not wishing to put-off the inevitable, the Colonel decided to remove his lifejacket at the earliest opportunity. Mostly though, he reflected on how close he had been to achieving his greatest success.

Conga was philosophical. Although he had failed in his quest to apprehend Smokey ... and was about to drown, he found himself content. The last few months had been the most stimulating of his life. The hunt for Smokey had made it so. It had fuelled his evil imagination ... the chase itself as well as the contemplation of sweet victory and her spoils.

Conga loved it ... and to die doing that which you love was all anybody could ask.

CHAPTER
TWENTY THREE

Moose had to do something.

It wasn't in him to do nothing ... to leave whoever was onboard the C catamaran to perish.

He scanned the storm beach.

From end to end, huge breakers pounded the shore, making it impossible to swim out.

'But what of the headland? At the North end of the cove?'

It extended beyond the surf line. Perhaps he could make it from there.

Moose sprinted over and where the beach met the limestone promontory he began to climb.

At the top, he turned left and started out towards the tip of the point.

It was slow going. The rocks were jagged and covered with razor sharp limpets. Time and again they sliced through the soles of his feet.

He didn't notice.

His thoughts were elsewhere ... at the end of the point ... and how, specifically, he could get from there into the water without being driven back by the swell.

It was a problem for sure, but one Moose himself would not have to answer. The solution presented itself when he next looked up.

'AAAAAGGGGHHHHH!!'

To his horror and despite the fact he was at least thirty feet above sea-level, Moose found himself staring skyward into the curl of a Rogue Wave.

Instantly, he dropped to his belly and with fingers and toes, clamped himself to the rock.

When the wave hit, it felt as if an Airship filled with wet poo had fallen onto his head.

Even so, Moose held firm. He sucked himself against the rock and with the strength of a stubborn stain, resisted the scourge of saltwater.

Trouble was, it kept coming. Even when the wave was gone, all that sea, so violently hurled from itself, had to return and soon it was draining off the point like a rapid, not only pulling at Moose with the strength of the preceding wave, but maintaining enough depth to keep him completely submerged.

Moose held on ... both to the rock and his dwindling breath.

His cheeks puffed out. They turned red. His eyes bulged. His cheeks turned blue. Then he could stand no more.

Moose relaxed his fingers.

'WHOOOSH!'

Next thing he knew, he was travelling at what felt like a thousand miles an hour ... sideways then down ... off the point.

He braced himself. Expecting to smash against rock.

'Any second now' he thought.

Instead, by some miracle, he landed with a splash.

Surfacing a split second later, Moose realised he was in the sea.

'YIPPEEEEEE!' he shouted and seizing his chance, Moose put his best paw forward and before the ocean had time to generate new bombardments, he doggie-paddled away from the point into deep water.

Once a safe distance away, Moose stopped swimming. 'Phew!' he gasped ... more from relief than breathlessness, before craning his head above the water to locate the catamaran.

Once spotted, Moose set off with renewed confidence. 'After all', he thought, 'it was probably no more than a mile away ... an easy distance ... what could possibly go wrong?'

****

Plenty .... that was what ... and more than likely caused by the cuts in his feet which left a trail of red behind him.

...and the trail told a tale ... a tale broadcast far and wide ... in mysterious particles of bloody saltwater travelling at lightning speed ... against swell, current and eddy to arrive, fresh as you like, into the nostrils of great big slobbery sharks.

****

Moose pulled alongside the upturned catamaran at exactly 9.45am.

The hulls were too slippery to scale, so he made his way to the stern, hauling himself up via the starboard rudder.

Once on top, a quick shimmy to the centre dagger board and Moose was secure.

He plotted his next move.

It occurred to him that anybody trapped within the boat might be alerted via a tap-tapping on the hull ...

... So that's what he did ...

... But there was no reply.

CHAPTER
TWENTY FOUR

The Colonel was alive.

Arcing through the air - his journey from boat to ocean-deep almost complete - Conga's arms had reached ahead, leading the rest of him through a dive.

The splashdown had been neat ... championship quality ... Conga's entire weight concentrated onto the tips of fingers and thumbs.

Unfortunately, before the water, those digits had encountered an unlikely piece of driftwood.

If the Colonel's thumb had pained him on the boat, well that pain was but a Cocktail Gherkin compared to the Cucumber of agony he experienced courtesy of a rusty nail protruding from the driftwood which impaled his thumb and ripped a lump of flesh clean off its already exposed bone.

Ironically, it was this that saved him.

So excruciating was the destruction of his thumb, it caused Conga to pass out thus confounding his plan to remove his lifejacket.

CHAPTER
TWENTY FIVE

Shirley was a shark and she was confused.

She had followed a path of blood ... but the path had forked.

So she turned left ... arriving seconds later alongside the most curious of fish ... a huge motionless fish with two bodies and what she could only describe as a mammalian protuberance onto which was attached a large white canvas flap.

Her bulging eyes fell on that protuberance.

'How strange' she thought 'It has ropes attached to it. Ooooh ... and its sooo stiff!'

Shirley blushed ...

... then she drooled ...

'Cooooeeeeerrr! Its longer than he is!'

... then lamented ...

'Pencil-like though!'

Shirley circled the fish for some minutes.

She eyed its length ... checking for signs of life ... assessing the possibility it may just be dozing. After all, the stiffness of its sausage surely indicated the creature was in the throes of a rather fruity dream.

But there was no movement. It just rolled lifelessly upon the swell.

Shirley steeled herself for an attack. She dove beneath the fish, turned and shot up towards what she best judged to be its head.

... but with just two metres between them, the fish made the strangest of noises ... a tap-tapping, which put the fear of Neptune into Shirley causing her to swerve violently, just missing the creature and breaching the ocean surface just one metre abaft of Primrose.

The instant she splashed down, Shirley turned tail and fled.

****

Moose stopped tapping.

The sight of a Tiger Shark, at least five metres from nose to tail, thrashing around in the same water from which, just seconds earlier he had emerged, was nearly enough to curdle his blood ...

... but not quite.

... it still flowed freely, a fact noted by Moose upon looking down and noticing, for the first time, the cuts in his feet and the blood pulsing out of them, down the side of the upturned hull and into the water.

'Doh!' ... he cursed before reverting his gaze back to the shark.

Moose followed its progress.

To his delight, it appeared to be swimming away.

'YIPPEEE!' thought Moose ... but just as quickly, he wondered why ... why it was leaving?

... and as he wondered, it changed direction.

Moose watched as it turned and swam a purposeful swim towards some point off Primrose's port beam. He extrapolated its course ... looking ahead until he saw where the shark was headed ... and not for the first time his eyes fell upon Colonel Conga.

****

Now, it must be said that Shirley's hunting routine, in shark terms at least, was about as mundane as a Muddlehead's trip on the Muddlehead Metro to the Muddlehead Mall.

Day in day out it involved little more than sneaking up on small fish.

When tackling a Savage Herring or a Man-eating Halibut, it was easy for Shirley to be a Tiger ... but anything else ... anything not falling within the ordinary presented her with a good deal of risk ... which to Shirley was unacceptable ... for despite her bulk, she was a delicate creature who worried over the smallest injury and how it could leave her vulnerable.

And that was the reason she turned so abruptly from Primrose and swam away.

Even so, Shirley was still hungry and with that in mind, she retraced her path along the trail of blood until once again she arrived at the point where it forked.

This time she changed course onto the second path and a couple of seconds later, in the distance, Shirley spotted the Colonel.

Cautiously, she swam closer. Shirley was still jittery from her last encounter so it took a while for her to muster the courage to come closer. When eventually she did, Shirley saw a rather nasty injury inflicted on the creature's left flipper.

'Magic!' she thought 'I might be in for a jolly feed after all!'

****

Moose, realising the mortal danger the floating man was in and without a second thought, hurled himself into the water and started to swim.

... And as he swum, Moose started to wonder.

'What the bloody hell am I doing? How am I gonna stop this shark?'

They were good questions and fortunately for Moose, several strokes later the answers popped into his head like sticky buns popping into the gaping gob of an obese child.

The answers he gleaned from a story ... a story he had once been told by Skipper Kipper.

As children, he and Fanny had been captivated by the rotund old rooster's constant supply of stories ... fantastical stories which nonetheless, according to Kipper, were based on truth ... including the tale of The Shark Matadors who lived on Twilisle a legendary island in the far eastern sea once visited by Kipper.

There, the crusty critter had noted how the Twilislanders, on a Sunday, enjoyed a nice feed of shark and how, in a most peculiar and foolhardy way, they went about the business of bagging one.

Armed with only a dagger, a usually sozzled islander, when the thought occurred to him, would swim out to sea ... and with a fair bit of splashing and squawking ... would endeavour to upset a Tiger Shark just enough for it to mount an attack.

Then came the part which Moose now found himself relying on.

According to Kipper, the Matadors had knowledge of a quirk peculiar to Tiger Sharks. Without fail, before striking their prey, they rolled onto their side. Extraordinary? ... Maybe not ... but maybe so considering the rolling was always in the same direction.

It gave a Twilislander the chance to dodge out of the way and with a free hand thrust his dagger into the shark's newly-exposed belly. What a mess! The shark's momentum coupled with its tender tum would cause the knife to slice from top to tail. For the shark, death was quick ... not so much from the loss of innards which under the circumstances, had a ghoulish tendency to burst free from the body, thus saving the native the tiresome task of later gutting his catch ... but from the shock ... of seeing those innards sink towards the seabed ... pursued by his very own family and friends who were not so concerned with his welfare as they were with stuffing their fat faces on the tripe that was once his tum!

For Moose, this was all very interesting as he powered through the water towards a point where he estimated he would intercept the shark. Alas though, the one part of the story which for the life of him he could not remember, was the most important part.

In which direction did a Tiger Shark roll?

Clockwise or counter-clockwise?

How vitally important the question. How else would he know which way to dodge or for that matter, in which hand to hold his knife?

Try as he might though, Moose could not recall.

CHAPTER TWENTY SIX

10:00am the time. The place ... a non-descript patch of ocean one nautical mile off the western shore of Moonshine.

Porcadillo the Pink-Toed Booby wheeled through the sky, observing as the scene unfolded below. His was the ideal vantage point ... the perfect position from which to provide a running commentary of events.

Unfortunately, Porcadillo did not have a microphone ...

... but if he had and had known the players' names, not forgetting the power of speech or a position within the Booby Broadcasting Company ... this is how he might have commented ...

'Colonel Conga is bleeding ... he's not moving ... HE'S UNCONSCIOUS! Wait ... Shirley the Shark has spotted him...

... she's swimming over.

WATCH OUT CONGA!

Hold on ... Shirley's changed course ...

...Shirley the Shark has changed course ... she's turning towards Moose!

... and Moose is swimming at a blistering pace ... TOWARDS SHIRLEY!

LOOK AT HIM GO!

What's this?

He's stopped

Moose has stopped dead in his tracks!

Wait ... what's he doing?

I DON'T BELIEVE IT!

Moose is squawking like a banshee!

Surely he's not trying to attract Shirley's attention?

He **IS** trying to attract Shirley's attention!

Uh oh ... that's done it.

Here comes Shirley ...

... and, oh boy ... does she look mad!

Here we go!

She's charging!

SHIRLEY IS CHARGING MOOSE!

Come on Moose ... get out the way!

MOOSE ... COME ON!

What's he doing?

Wait! What's that in his left hand?

IT'S A KNIFE! ... MOOSE HAS A KNIFE!

Now it's in his right ... no ... its back in his left.

He seems confused.

OH NO! HE'S FUMBLED IT! MOOSE HAS DROPPED THE KNIFE! IT'S SINKING!

He's in for it now!

But what's this?

AN INVADER ON THE PITCH!

My word ... it's a Dolphin!

What's it doing?

Surely not.

I DON'T BELIEVE IT!

IT'S CHARGING SHIRLEY!

WHOOAAA!

IT'S HIT SHIRLEY...THE DOLPHIN HAS HIT SHIRLEY!

Shirley's lashing out with her tail.

OUCH! The Dolphin's hit!

THAT'S GOTTA HURT!

The Dolphin's injured ... it's swimming away.

Hold on ... SO IS SHIRLEY!

THE DOLPHIN AND SHIRLEY ARE RETREATING ... IN OPPOSITE DIRECTIONS!

Oh well sports fans ... it's a funny old game!'

... and that was that.

Moose and Conga were spared from the jaws of Shirley the Shark by a dolphin ... a dolphin who appeared from nowhere and disappeared just as quick.

But that wasn't the end of it.

Moose still had to get himself and Conga to shore.

And what a struggle that proved ...

... a lengthy saga to be sure and not one which can be told with any justice within the limited space afforded by these pages. Not room to describe how the brave fellow fought a legion of Shirley's smaller relatives, snapping at his bloody feet and Conga's bloodier thumb ... nor time to illustrate the fantastic spectacle of a life jacketed human surfboard ridden expertly by Moose down the face of a humungous wave and navigated between sharp rocks to the safety of the beach.

No, these things cannot be told ... for the time has come to move on!

CHAPTER
TWENTY SEVEN

It was quite a while before the Colonel came to on that Morningtarian Storm beach. In the meantime, Moose sewed up the fellow's injured thumb with copra twine and a sharpened sea urchin spine.

Then Moose decided to make a fire - to warm his soggy patient - so off he went in search of firewood.

While Moose was gone, the Colonel woke up.

Conga, once he had come to his senses, looked down at his lifejacket ... and over, to the man collecting driftwood above the high-tide mark.

... and he understood.

All things considered, and despite the pain in his thumb, Conga was absolutely chuffed. He recognised Moose ... but more important ... was sure that Moose did not recognise him. If that had been the case ... if the memory of dream had focussed into the recollection of real events ... of Conga in the Interview Room, then surely Moose would have left him to the fish.

Heading back to the stranger, Moose was surprised to see him on his feet. He dropped his driftwood and ran over.

The Colonel, tottering about on unsure land-legs, was struggling to remove his lifejacket.

'Not so fast' called Moose 'I'll help you with that.'

He reached the Colonel and helped him unbuckle the vest.

'You should sit down' he continued 'You've been through an ordeal.'

'No! No!' countered Conga 'I'm perfectly alright.'

When they had stopped fussing (as strangers always do in such situations), they looked each other over.

Conga held out his good hand ...

'I'm Cer - Cerr - CUCUMBER!' he stammered 'It is - sniff sniff - a great honour to meet - sniff sniff snivel - the man who has single-handedly saved my life!' Then he made great ceremony of simultaneously breaking down, hugging the man who he found to be called Moose and sobbing uncontrollably.

Moose was not inclined to return the Colonel's hug.

'Forget it.' he replied.

CHAPTER
TWENTY EIGHT

Fanny did not return to Look-at-Me Lagoon the same way she had come ... having no desire to negotiate the swamp.

Instead, she headed West, along a valley which reached the coast a couple of miles to the south.

It was a roundabout way home ... long but pleasant ... following a stream.

Some ways along - about a mile or so - the path crossed, via stepping stones, from one side of the stream to the other. Fanny took the opportunity to stop for a drink.

The water was lovely - rainfall from the previous night ... crystal clear - not yet corrupted by the earth - reflecting back at Fanny in her return to the sea.

When she had drunk, Fanny slid, fully clothed, into the water. It rushed over her ... cool and soothing ... a healing balm for a sore body ... and tortured mind. Fanny turned over. The water slid beneath her dress ... lifting coarse material until it no longer touched but floated, like white satin - opaque in the breeze. She arched her back ... luxuriating ... eyes closed ... neck stretched ... hair flowing down to the water.

'Mmmm' she sighed

Then opened her eyes...

'FIDDLESTICKS!' she cursed.

Fanny saw the sun. It was high in the sky ... almost midday.

'Oh well ... better be getting along ... Smokey and Kipper will be back by now.'

She pulled herself out of the water and in no time at all was off again.

****

On the stroke of midday, Fanny reached the coast.

The path from the Scooberry Patch came to a halt on a cliff top next to where the stream fell, unhindered, to the beach two hundred feet below.

Fanny looked over the edge.

Her eyes followed an old goat track. It was treacherous. In places, it had worn away ... but it was the only way down.

She concentrated - scanning its every twist and turn - checking to see if it was passable.

Her gaze reached the beach. She saw something else.

Two figures ... Moose and a stranger.

She saw what was happening ... and screamed.

CHAPTER
TWENTY NINE

The Colonel and Moose set off towards Look-at Me Lagoon and the Fishing Platform.

'Come on' said Moose in an upbeat, almost jovial tone 'We'll get you some food and figure out how to get you home.'

'We?' thought the Colonel. 'Hmmm.'

... And hastily surmised the 'we' almost certainly included Smokey Kingfish.

Conga's heart missed a beat

'This is it!' he thought 'I've got the little brat! He's holed up with Moose at Look-at-Me Lagoon!'

Inwardly, The Colonel danced a merry jig. His great quest was nearly at an end. All that was left was to get rid of the fool Moose and then ... sure as Sausage slides into Soufflé, Kingfish was his ... served up on a plate like the Stuck Pig he would surely become.

****

Whilst Conga silently rejoiced his good fortune, Moose, on the contrary, was feeling rather unhappy. He felt weird ... weird being around someone who so recently had been through so much.

'For heaven's sake' thought Moose, 'Cucumber nearly drowned and he's lost his boat ... what a bummer! What do you say to such a person?'

'Blowed if I know' Moose concluded ... so he kept his mouth shut.

Some minutes later, Conga ... err CUCUMBER, having had ample time to come up with a suitable ruse to lure Moose even more off-guard, broke the silence when he started to sob. Next minute, the cunning devil began to explain a manufactured version of who he was and what had happened ... how he had sailed from his home, an island many weeks to the West; how his chart had not revealed Moonshine; and how he'd hit a submerged reef. Cucumber told of his attempt to row ashore in a life raft with his wife and two small children. How they were set upon by a shark and how his family had been torn to pieces ... before his very eyes.

'Unbelievable!' thought Moose 'and I thought Cucumber was upset because he'd lost his boat!'

Then he thought some more ... and as he did, as the memory of his own tragedy came back to him, Moose's emotion began to change ... ghosts from the past.

He sat down, began to cry and through the tears was able to tell Cucumber his own sorry story.

He told the stranger everything ... all about Sundowner and his own family.

The words flooded out and all the while Moose wondered why ... why, in contrast to his usual self, he could be so open.

'Who is this man?' he thought 'Who is this man I can speak with so freely?'

Deep down he knew.

Cucumber was himself, or at least Cucumber's experience, at that moment, were the same as his.

Kindred spirits.

And afterwards ... after pouring out his heart, Moose sat with his head held in his hands. If before he'd felt uncomfortable - well that was a mere peanut compared to the pumpkin of discomfort he now felt.

Even so, despite the embarrassment, Moose felt strangely relieved - as if in the telling his burden had been lifted.

****

The Colonel looked at Moose.

'Strange kid' ... he thought ... but didn't stop to wonder why the boy had reacted so.

He wasn't interested.

Indeed, Conga had no interest in the reason for much of anything ... lest it got in the way of action. When opportunity arose, rather than ponder, he was straight at it ... like a short-sighted dog presented with a swaying vision of loveliness.

With Moose off-guard - head bowed in deep reflection - Conga grabbed a sturdy piece of driftwood, lifted it high and with calculated force, smashed it down across the back of the lad's head, knocking him out cold.

Afterwards, the Colonel sat down and paused for thought.

'Should I have waited?' he asked himself. 'What if Kingfish isn't at the Lagoon? How will I find him without Moose?'

Such thoughts however, coming after the fact, were academic and Conga shrugged them off.

He wasn't overly concerned because he was sure of what he would find at the Lagoon and besides, he was now able to reason, it was far safer to get Moose out of the way before confronting Kingfish.

He got up, walked over to the comatose Moose and kicked him hard in the ribs.

For the Colonel, the next few hours would reveal what his own vision of loveliness might be ... and even if it turned into a postman's leg ... no worries ... he'd get his rocks off anyway.

****

When he came to, Moose found himself staring into a hole.

It was growling.

'Aaargh!' screamed Moose, convinced in his groggy state the hole was a huge monster's mouth.

'Aaargh!' he screamed again, sure the growling sound was the monster's tum rumbling in anticipation.

'Aaargh!' he screamed once more, just before a high pressure jet of saltwater whooshed out of the hole, hitting him square in the chops.

Moose was knocked backwards and landed with a bonk.

'Ha! Ha!' laughed Conga ... who had been watching the whole time.

Moose tried to stand but discovered his hands and feet were bound.

'What the thwuck haff you done!' he spluttered at the Colonel.

Conga feigned surprise.

'Who?... Me?' he asked innocently before walking over to the hole which, it turned out, was nothing so exciting as a Monster's Mouth, but a Blowhole ... formed by a vertical fissure in the rock and connected to the sea via a horizontal lava tube.

Conga peered down.

The fissure was fractured and narrow - in places only three feet wide.

The tunnel it led to, however, was high and wide as a man. It ran for some fifty feet towards the sea, emerging slightly above the high tide-mark on a wave-swept ledge.

'Hmmm ... pretty impressive' the Colonel said to no one in particular before turning his attention back to Moose.

'Not wearing your uniform today?' he started.

Moose was slow to catch on.

'What the bloody-hell are you talking about ... you PSYCHO!'

'Now now' taunted Conga 'you don't mean to tell me you've lost it?'

Moose was confused.

Conga continued 'I can understand if you'd lost something small ... say a, err ... SAILOR'S CAP! ... But a whole ENFORCER'S UNIFORM? ... my ... my ... how very clumsy!'

A spark of recognition ignited inside Moose's head.

'DOH!' he thought.

The Colonel, noticing Moose's reaction, sidled over to his prisoner and calmly kicked him in the stomach before leaning down, grabbing him by the hair and snarling into his face ...

'Where's Kingfish you SLAG!?'

'UP YOURS!' countered Moose ... and instantly, an image of the Bongo bar flashed before him ... recollections of the last time he had uttered those words.

Moose flinched ... a remembrance of pain overwhelming him ... and prophecy of likewise to come.

'No matter' grinned the Colonel 'I'm sure I'll catch up with him.'

And with that, he dragged Moose back over to the edge of the blowhole.

On cue, a tremendous jet of water shot skyward.

It was a magnificent spectacle and Conga, overcome with excitement, danced a merry jig in the shower that followed. He also began to sing ... deranged renditions of Muddlehead folk tunes ... 'Shower time for two' ... 'Plip-Plop Mrs Mop'.

He sang with a manic gusto ...

'Plip-Plop Mrs Mop
Tell me where's your hub?
Plip-Plop Mrs Mop
Is he down the pub?
Come in from the rain ... till he's back again
What you need's a scrub
In me bathroom tub!'

'YOU - ARE - A - FREAK !' screamed Moose.

'YIPPEEEEE!' countered Conga as he continued to sing and splash about in the shallow rock pools.

Finally, he turned once again to Moose, flashed him a cheeky grin, raised his good arm, finger tapped a dainty 'bye - bye' and raised his right foot.

Moose braced himself and managed to absorb most of the Colonel's kick. Even so, it knocked him off balance. Moose's upper body teetered over the precipice and whilst his legs strained to pull him upright ... it was to no avail and he toppled backwards into the blowhole.

As Moose fell, instinctively he twisted his body and as luck would have it, the motion caused the rope which bound his feet to snag on a jagged overhang. It created a pivot point around which Moose swung, like the hands of a clock, from midday into the solid six o'clock of the blowhole wall.

'SPLAT!'... went his nose as he came to a dead halt ... suspended upside down like a Fruit Bat.

Seeing what had happened, the Colonel reacted quickly.

He took his knife, crouched down and cut the rope.

The delay was all Moose needed. As he fell for the second time, with his liberated feet, Moose sprung against the blowhole wall and like a cat, launched from an upstairs window by a naughty child, flipped his body thus avoiding a head first landing.

Nevertheless, Moose landed hard ... on his left side. He felt his arm shatter from the impact. It didn't slow him though. He leapt to his feet, took a quick look around, decided which way to run and took a step...

CHAPTER THIRTY

Rusty the Starfish was just that ... a Star.

She also happened to call a little crevice in the floor of the blowhole her home and whilst it was quite possibly the last place on earth a human might wish to find himself, to Rusty, a celebrated cabaret singer, it offered the one thing she craved the most ...

Peace.

When she wasn't residing in the blowhole, Rusty performed at 'The Seabed' ... a groovy joint frequented by a beatnik bunch of inebriate invertebrates including, coincidentally, our old friend Bert the Octopus who had recently upped tentacles and moved to the area.

Even more strange, Rusty had been forced to move into the blowhole in order to get away from Bert, who, ever since his bloody amputation at the hands of Moose, had turned into a drunken letch.

Indeed, Bert couldn't quite get enough of Rusty's soulful bubble blowing and arm dancing. He was obsessed with her and the more Rusty spurned his advances, the lewder and more intimidating Bert's propositions became ...

'Could you do it with a cripple?' he would ask, waving his stump in her face as she made her way to the stage ... and then, halfway through her act, as she blew fizzy sonnets to the audience, Bert would barge his way to the front of the crowd, shoot his muck all over the stage and scream to Rusty 'FANCY A GOOD OLD INKING LOVE?'

Bert was a scumbag to be sure and Rusty didn't deserve his abuse.

Another thing she didn't deserve was a premature end ... but that was what she got when Bert's disarming nemesis, Moose, stood on her.

CHAPTER THIRTY ONE

'Splodge ... Slippetty slip .... Whoa .....BONK!'

Moose lay on his back on the Blowhole floor ... covered in a sludge of dead starfish.

And as he lay there, he listened ...

To the roar of an approaching wave.

Next moment, Moose found himself shooting skywards out of the blowhole into sunlight.

At an altitude of one hundred feet, he stopped. For a split second, Moose was afforded a marvellous gull's eye view of the surrounding coast and the magnificent waterfall which emerged from the lush rainforest to his right.

'Oh, isn't that nice' thought Moose before starting his descent. But something else caught his eye ... a figure standing at the top of the waterfall, waving her arms and screaming.

Moose recognised his sister. He was surprised to see her but was more concerned by the obvious distress she was in. 'What on earth could be wrong?' he wondered.

Seeing as she was looking straight back at him, it was rather a silly question.

Seconds later, Moose landed, or more precisely, splashed down.

What luck! Firstly the fellow had survived being shot from the blowhole. Second, by an absolute fluke, his angle of ascent had taken him seaward thus depositing him into an ocean cushioned by the foaming residue of spent waves.

Unfortunately for Moose, that was where his luck ran out.

CHAPTER
THIRTY TWO

'Ooh! My head!'

It was late morning and Bert had just woken up ... with a hangover.

'I shwall never dwink again!' he quietly resolved ... before stretching out an involuntary arm to fondle Rusty.

But she wasn't there. He was still dreaming. Rusty wasn't beside him in his love grotto and what's more, in the cold plankton-filtered light of day, as Bert gradually came round, morning's sober reality told him she never would be.

'I'm sho alone!' he sobbed pathetically.

Oh yes. Bert was a wreck. A mere shell of his former self and what's more, he knew it. He knew because the contrast between how he was now and how he used to be, was so stark ... so blatantly clear. Bert had become twisted and filled with guile ... and his bitterness was all directed toward one object ... the human being .... 'That scum what maimed me!' as Bert succinctly put it.

Of course, the human being to which Bert referred was Moose, and as coincidence would have it, that very moment Moose was a mere twenty one feet above Bert ... and closing fast.

SPLASH!

'What was that?' Bert looked up, half expecting to see a shark bearing down on him.

When he did manage to focus, his eyes nearly popped out of their sockets. On the surface, a mere twenty feet above him, was a man ... one he recognised.

'B-B-B-BLOODY 'ELL ... ITS THAT HUMAN!!' he spluttered.

As Moose bobbed up and down in the surf, marvelling at his own good fortune, he felt something wrap around his legs. Then slowly and quite deliberately, he was drawn down ... into the depths.

There was no struggle. Moose's arms were still bound and this time, he had no knife.

For Bert the Octopus, revenge most certainly was a dish best served cold.

CHAPTER
THIRTY THREE

Whilst the aforementioned drama was unfolding; four nautical miles further out to sea, a tanned, rather skinny young man was sitting impatiently in a leaky old outrigger.

Smokey Kingfish's furrowed brow and clenched jaw betrayed a growing anguish.

He was worried. Where could the Skipper be? It was almost midday and he'd been awaiting the blubbery one's return for a good six hours.

Smokey looked down ... at the huge Tuna Fish lolling lifelessly around the bilge.

Despite his initial enthusiasm, Smokey had never got around to gutting and filleting his catch.

'Doh!' he thought. 'It's gonna go rotten if we don't get back soon.'

CHAPTER
THIRTY FOUR

Colonel Conga watched with glee as his latest victim disappeared under the water. He watched for as long as necessary to satisfy himself Moose was gone.

Then slowly, deliberately, Conga turned and looked up ... towards the top of the waterfall ... towards the sound of screaming ... towards Fanny.

He started to move away from the shore towards the base of the cliff, all the time keeping the girl in his sight.

Fanny saw the Colonel out of the corner of her eye. She fell quiet. Her mind ... all of a jumble just a few seconds earlier ... suddenly focussing.

'Moose is dead.' ... she made herself think the unthinkable truth ... confronted it and by doing so, put it to the back of her mind.

Then, she shifted her gaze ... away from the ocean towards her brother's killer.

From a distance of three hundred yards, even though she could not see them, she sensed his eyes, sensed his gaze meet hers ... sensed the evil ... taking up residence in her soul.

Quickly, Fanny turned away. She steadied herself ... mustered up a calm resolve ... to banish the hate ... and just like that, it was gone ... just as quickly as it had arrived.

Suddenly she was cool. Her thoughts collected and focused on what was to come.

The Killer has started to climb the cliff. He was after her. She thought about Smokey and Kipper. Her goodness, at that very moment, did not look to them for protection ... on the contrary ... she looked to protect them ... to lead the killer away. Reason took over. If Moose had returned then so had the SS Bulldog. There was only one thing for it. To get away, she had to make it to the other side of the island ... to the SS Bulldog.

Fanny knew it was her only chance.

****

Despite the near vertical distance between them and despite the care it would take to negotiate such a treacherous cliff path, Fanny knew she only had a quarter-hour start on the Colonel ... at the most.

Even at a run, it would take at least four hours to cross over to the East coast of Moonshine ... to the small bay where she hoped her dear brother had left the SS Bulldog.

There was absolutely no margin for error but Fanny did not allow herself to ponder on that.

She was fit and she knew the way. That was all that mattered.

Fanny turned back to the path from whence she'd come and started to run ...

... and run ... and run.

****

An hour later, she was still going ... her pace steady ... steely gaze fixed on the track ahead ... all the time resolving to ignore the pain that was her only companion. Denying herself any hurt ... either emotional ... from the thought of her lost brother ... or physical ... from blistered feet and aching limbs. Nothing to distract her as she raced onwards and upwards toward the Volcano ... her gateway to the far side of Moonshine and safety.

Fanny's pace never slowed. It only seemed so. Lower down, the trail had been narrow ... trees and ferns crowding in from either side. She had whizzed passed them ... ducking low branches, hurdling logs and stones. So closed in ... every step a bullet reaction to changing terrain.

It had all been a blur and the apparent speed had sustained and encouraged her onwards.

But now, as Fanny moved into the open ground on the lower slopes of the Volcano, she began to feel slow and vulnerable.

A high pasture ascended for half a mile before giving way to the screed at the base of the Volcano. Here, a forest had once stood. But fire had claimed it leaving nothing but a verdant carpet of buffalo grass in place of the trees.

The terrain offered Fanny no encouragement ... nothing to whiz through ... nothing to pace herself against. The crater rim was her next destination but it was too far ... too stationary ... to provide a sensation of progress. Instead, Fanny stared downwards ... trying to achieve the same uplifting sensation of speed by watching the rush of grass beneath her feet.

It only made her dizzy.

'Still so far to go' she agonised before stealing a glance over her shoulder ... back to a point where the jungle ended and the pasture began.

No sign of 'THE BEAST'.

She had not seen him since that dreadful moment looking down from the waterfall.

Fanny did not know how far behind he was ... but she knew for certain he was there. He was on her tail. He was tracking her down. THE BEAST WAS THERE.

And then she fell ... not looking where she was going, you see.

So clumsy.

It was nothing serious, mind ... just a few scratches. However, it gave fatigue a chance to catch and overtake her. Fanny was exhausted ... devoid of all strength, she was unable to lift herself straight back up.

Instead she returned her gaze back towards the jungle.

She was drawn to look for what she hoped was not there ...

BUT HE WAS.

Conga burst free from the jungle.

He looked ahead ... towards his quarry.

She was only a couple of hundred yards ahead ... lying on the ground staring back at him.

'Has she given up?' he wondered.

No such luck.

As Conga looked on, the girl clambered to her feet and moved off.

'Damn you!' he cursed.

'Do us all a favour and stay put!'

But that was a wasted wish. Fanny was not about to give up.

Once again, the Colonel was forced to take up the chase and whilst he was tired, unfortunately for Fanny, he was not as tired as she was.

Up the meadow they raced. Conga bounding forwards with long purposeful strides ... Fanny, frantically scampering on unsteady legs.

Quickly, the two hundred yards between them turned to one hundred and fifty ... and by the time the grass under Fanny's feet gave way to screed, her lead was cut by half.

Frantically, she clambered up the unstable rock towards the Volcano's summit. The climb was impossibly hard work and time and again Fanny's progress was stymied when her feet fell away and she was left clawing at the pumice rock with bare hands.

... and all the time, the Colonel was coming up fast ... in for the kill.

Fanny became frantic. Tears welling up in her eyes as she struggled harder against the confounding rock.

The Colonel was nearly on her.

She could hear him behind her now. Hear the crunch of his feet ... his grunting and his curses.

Finally ...

... she heard a rumble.

Fanny stumbled ... only this time it wasn't just the screed beneath her feet which moved.

This time it was the whole flamin' Volcano!

As she began to slide back down the slope, Fanny realised with horror that she was caught in the middle of an earthquake ...

... and in the split second before her mind turned its whole attention to the task of taking best care of her body, she once again concluded that it was all down to her ... that Moonshine was picking on her.

Indeed, it was delivering Fanny straight into the hands of her pursuer.

Was Moonshine siding with the Colonel?

Well ... whether it was or not was a mute point and what's more, the beastly Conga certainly didn't feel as if he was being advantaged.

Indeed, catching the girl suddenly became the very last thing he wanted to do.

Instead, the nasty old noodle, who most definitely was not keen on becoming a human skittle - especially when Fanny, the equally human bowling ball, was being helped along by several tonnes of loose rock - endeavoured to get out of her way.

But to no avail.

The swiftly descending Fanny hit him square in the midriff.

... and what's more ... the two of them ended up in a clinch ...tangled together like a pair of stinky socks stuffed into a ball at the bottom of a stinky sock drawer.

'AAAARGGHHHH!' screamed Conga.

'EEEEEIIIIGGHHH!' squealed Fanny.

... and downwards they tumbled ... swept along on a tide of vibrating rubble until slowly it thinned around them, and they came to a gentle stop in the soft grass of the pasture.

Five seconds. That was all it had taken to fall at least three hundred feet.

Still, it could have been a lot worse.

Just as quickly as the earthquake had started ... then it stopped and with it the landslide.

Fanny and Conga were shocked and bewildered. They still clung onto one another ... as if having survived a most terrible ordeal was reason enough to forget the last couple of hours.

Neither felt inclined to let the other go.

They examined one another.

Both the Colonel and Fanny were sporting a large number of cuts and bruises ... superficial but nonetheless quite painful.

Involuntarily, the Colonel took hold of Fanny's arm. He did not grab ... but lifted it gently ... examining a nasty cut on the girl's hand.

For her part, Fanny did not resist.

Then, in unison, their attention turned to their surroundings.

Where, a few moments earlier, the earth had been in turmoil, now, an eerie calm descended.

All around, a fine dust hung in the air, muffling both sight and sound and thrusting Fanny and the Colonel into a half-world of echo and silhouette where the only object each could determine was the other.

Conga turned back to Fanny ... studying the expression on her face.

It was not as he suspected it might be. There was no fear in her eyes ... only a questioning bewilderment. It was the same expression Fanny had worn earlier that morning in the Scooberry Patch when she had agonised over Moonshine's conspiracy against her.

It seemed to Conga that she was pleading to him.

Not for mercy ... but comfort.

Despite all that had happened, Conga and Fanny, for a moment at least, found an ally in one another.

They were, after all, in the same boat.

CHAPTER
THIRTY FIVE

The Volcano's silence lasted thirty five whole seconds. The thirty sixth brought with it a second rumble ... a low pitched rumble. By the thirty seventh, the rumble had grown louder. The thirty eighth, it was louder still ... and closer. The thirty ninth, the ground started to shake. The fortieth and .... BOOM!

Conga and Fanny looked skyward ... their heads tilting and jaws dropping in unison.

'Blow me! The Volcano! It's erupted!' gasped Fanny.

And she was right!

The molten lava skyrocketing out of the crater proved it.

Conga was quick to react. He grabbed Fanny by the waist, tucked her neatly under his arm and began to run.

He started down the hillside ... legs turning cartwheels in the rush. His round eyes, like oranges, peeled ... skirting the terrain in search of shelter.

It did not take long to find.

As the first humungous wads of lava began to splatter the ground around them, Conga dodged into a handy cave.

Once inside, he put Fanny down.

Immediately she retreated to the far corner while he remained at the entrance ... staring out in terrified wonder.

Conga looked onto an apocalyptic scene.

Above his head, the air was turned to an infernal soup.

Fireballs of molten rock fizzed by, scorching deep red trails through a dense, suspended ash. It transformed the half light into shredded twilight ... streaks of blood in the devil's bubbling cauldron.

The image of hell was not lost on Conga.

As he stood watching, Conga came to the stark realisation that he and the girl were doomed and what's more, for him at least ... eternal damnation was waiting.

He felt sick ... as if his heart had been wrenched into the pit of his stomach, to leave just a hollow empty space.

It wasn't that Conga feared death, mind you. Or hell for that matter.

That was not what overcame him.

No ... his thoughts had returned to Smokey Kingfish.

His despair came because he knew the hunt was finally done ... that Smokey, his arch rival, would remain forever out of reach.

But what of Kingfish? Had Conga's intuition served him true?

Now, at least, he had the means to find out ... to discover if Smokey Kingfish had come to Moonshine.

Conga turned to Fanny.

At this stage, both their fates were sealed and if, as he was sure, the girl knew of Smokey, surely she would tell him as much ... for the perverse satisfaction of telling a sweet fortune to one whose greater misfortune turns it sour.

He saw her cowering, terrified at the back of the Cave and walked the ten paces over to her. He crouched down and immediately saw the anguish in her eyes.

Fanny was looking towards the Cave entrance.

When she finally turned to him, once again it seemed to Conga that her eyes were pleading to him for comfort ... as if she were a small child, scared ... not of the person in front of her, but rather ... looking to him for strength.

'Surely she hasn't forgotten the blowhole?' wondered Conga.

'No matter.' he concluded.

Then gently, he took Fanny's shivering hand and looked her straight in the eye.

'Sweetheart.' he asked 'Do you know a fellow by the name of Smokey Kingfish?'.

Given their present predicament, it must have seemed to Fanny an entirely mistimed and irrelevant question.

She didn't reply.

Instead, Fanny lowered her eyes.

The Colonel was wearing the same cotton shirt he had worn to his bunk the previous evening. It had barely survived the trials of the last eighteen hours. Torn and ragged, the shirt was hardly appropriate attire for a Chief Morningtarian Enforcement Officer.

Such trivia was lost on Fanny. She did not look to the Colonel's shirt ... but beyond ... to his musky, angular chest.

And as quickly as that, lust took over. Sober peril drowned by a single wayward glance.

Fanny reached up and started to claw at the shirt.

Conga was taken aback.

'Is she attacking me?'

His confusion lasted only briefly.

He soon caught up.

After all, what time did they have?

... and soon enough, it wasn't the deafening malevolence beyond the cave that Conga and Fanny heard ... but the sound of shortened breath ... and ripping fabric.

In a second, they were naked ... Conga stamping on his pants, prising them clear of his feet; Fanny, with her dress, doing likewise before leaping onto him ... straddling his waist.

Conga supported her weight easily. After all, she was half his size. He bent his knees and sunk to the ground ... the girl underneath him, and by the time the ground was against her back, he was inside her.

A second later ... they were trapped.

Not that it really mattered.

Conga and Fanny no longer cared ... didn't even notice when the end came.

... the red hot tongue of lava, licking at the mouth of the cave ... skirting the rim ... edging deeper ... penetrating ... probing each corner ... every crevice ... scorching heat upon writhing bodies ... consummation ... welcome hellfire ... burnt flesh melting together.

Good and evil fused by fire ... into one.

CHAPTER THIRTY SIX

As a large minority of the human race might have expected, when the Colonel and Fanny died, their spirits ascended from out of scorched bodies.

They were set free, for the time being at least, from the shackles of a human existence.

And just as their flesh had melted and merged into one ... so too did their spirits.

Fanny and Conga became soul mates.

Who would have thought it?

Well, you might recall, the Skipper had ... the previous evening in the telling of his three truths.

At the time, he had greatly upset Fanny by questioning the sacred certainty of another's love ... more specifically, her love for Smokey Kingfish.

'Smokey is not your soul mate' Kipper had said 'this man you will meet with shortly ...he will make you complete.'

The man to whom Kipper referred was Colonel Conga and, by-Jove, he certainly had made the girl complete ... as complete as one half of anything can be ... when it discovers its other.

And so it was ... in a world with not enough souls to go around, Fanny was destined to share hers ... and a convergence so created formed at once a holy alliance and at the same time a battle forever more.

Potent duality ... Good and Evil ... on each other's tail for all eternity ... whirling across the universe ... outwards towards the frontiers of all knowledge ... towards enlightenment ... and back again.

CHAPTER
THIRTY SEVEN

Earlier that same day, Smokey's so recently fried girlfriend had been of the opinion that her scorched toes were a direct result of Moonshine's conspiracy against her.

Perhaps if that frazzled young lady had possessed the scientific faculties of a Vulcanologist, her deductions might have been less personal.

After all, acidic swamps and boiling springs were clearly non-emotional, geological signs that Moonshine's dormant Volcano was returning to life.

But what about Smokey?

What might he have concluded in Fanny's place?

Well, he knew even less about such things.

Despite having nearly died in the Volcano's crater his first week on the island and despite the Volcano's geographic dominance over Moonshine ... Smokey had barely given it a second thought.

The Volcano, after all, was always behind him.

Smokey looked towards the sea ... not the earth.

That was until 1:35pm.

When he heard the boom, Smokey nearly fell overboard from the outrigger.

He twisted round ... towards where the sound was coming ... towards the island.

Smokey was at least five nautical miles out to sea ... still waiting for Kipper to return to the outrigger.

Despite his distance from Moonshine, the eruption was so loud, it felt to Smokey as if his ear drums had burst.

Pain was soon forgotten, however. The spectacle before Smokey was so awe-inspiring, he might not even have noticed if the dead Tuna by his feet had reincarnated itself, picked up the fishing pole and shoved it up his bum!

'WOW!' screamed Smokey 'this is MAGIC!' and he danced around the boat like a small child.

It was a typical reaction. Smokey's imagination running away with him.

Smokey was beside himself, not with anxiety, but wonder.

'WOW!' he marvelled once again. 'This is AT LEAST ten times better than last year's Bobo Street Fireworks Display!'

Smokey was positively brimming with excitement, even more so when his thoughts turned to Fanny.

'Cor, I bet she has a magic view!'

Even more typical.

Not for one second did the happy go lucky young rooster consider the mortal danger Fanny, or for that matter, Kipper or himself, were in.

But that quickly changed.

The next second, the eruption itself was engulfed ... by an explosion. A blast so huge, so powerful, it caused the whole of Moonshine to disintegrate ...

... and Smokey to soil his pants.

CHAPTER
THIRTY EIGHT

Bobby the Booby, after witnessing the dramatic stand-off between Moose and Shirley the Shark, had continued unperturbed onwards to his favourite fishing grounds. Once there, he had located then gorged himself on a large shoal of sardines before returning, suitably stuffed, to his roost on Moonshine's West coast.

As coincidence would have it, Bobby lived beside the waterfall, in the same cliff upon which Fanny, at the very moment of his return, had been standing. Bobby had spotted her just as the sea below him had given way to the rocky coastal strip. Then Bobby had spotted someone else ... another human ... this time a man ... flying swiftly towards him.

Lucky for Bobby his reactions had been good, otherwise he might not have been able to dodge the man ... a young man he recognised as Moose.

Afterwards, Bobby had circled above the scene just long enough to be sure of Moose's demise before returning once more to sea, to report the sad news to a friend of his.

****

Kipper could do no more. After hearing the news, he turned and headed back towards the outrigger. It was a long, lonely swim. He had known all along but nevertheless was devastated by the Booby's confirmation. Kipper was grief stricken. After all, Moose had been like a son to him.

As Kipper swam, his arm started to hurt. He recognised the pain as a remembrance ... a link between him and Moose. The lad's arm had been broken in the blowhole ... and Kipper's ... during his encounter with Shirley the Shark.

Kipper had sustained his injury saving Moose only for the lad to be killed just a few hours later. It was as if the one injury had been a physical prophecy of the other.

For Kipper, as he struggled back to Smokey and the outrigger, it was almost too much to bear. Despite his wisdom; despite his high-brow spiritualism, Kipper found himself overcome with earthly grief and human pain.

It was a lesson he embraced.

To feel human.

Duality, after all, did not just exist between good and evil ... it also existed between the earthbound and spiritual ... between angels and acolytes ... men and their Gods. Ultimately, it was why those journeys undertaken by Kipper and Watersplash had come full circle, returning them to the physical world.

They had come back because they needed to.

****

Kipper collected himself and climbed aboard the outrigger.

Smokey, who was sitting on the bowsprit, did not notice the old man.

He was too preoccupied ... gazing dumbfounded at the huge dust cloud which was emerging from out of the sea where the island of Moonshine had once stood.

Smokey did not hear the Skipper either. His ears were still numb from the Volcano's explosion ... a blast so loud it was heard in the cities of Morningtaria a thousand miles to the south where a million housewives mistook it for a thunderstorm thus causing them to rush in unison into their backyards to bring in the washing.

****

Smokey felt an arm rest on his shoulder and turned towards Kipper.

'Prepare yourself' said the old fellow.

'For what?' asked Smokey

'For that' answered Kipper, pointing over Smokey's shoulder.

Smokey turned back towards the dust cloud.

He looked and saw the ocean.

Trouble was, his head was bent back and his eyes were pointing skyward.

Those dopey Morningtarian housewives would be proved right after all. Their washing would get wet ... whether left on the clothes line or put in the airing cupboard. The humungous tidal wave bearing down on Smokey and Kipper would see to that.

Conceived by the earthly upheaval of Moonshine, it was huge ... at least a thousand feet high and growing. Once it had time to draw the ocean into itself, it would get bigger ... and faster. In less than five minutes the wave would reach the coast of Morningtaria.

... and in less than four minutes, those Morningtarians residing by the sea would observe the tide as it receded with such pace and for such a distance, it would appear as if the beach itself had chased the sea over the horizon, replacing it with a soggy moonscape of rock, sand and stranded fish. That is, until a minute later when it would return. At lightning speed the tide would return ... on a surge so high it would reach to the clouds and engulf the whole of Morningtaria. The tidal wave would flatten that Dark Continent and sweep away its entire population. Bosspigs and Bongoball Supporters alike. None would escape its wrath and when it was done, everything would be calm and once again, the fish would lay claim to the land ... a billion fold scaly bottom feeders gorging on the rotten carcass of Morningtaria ... a lost civilisation.

CHAPTER
THIRTY NINE

In every suburb and village of Morningtaria, for those millions of Muddelhead housewives, another day of domestic bliss was beginning.

Even for Bernice Biff.

Despite the momentous changes which had occurred the last few months, it was business as usual.

Smokey had gone ... and Bubba too. But they would be back ... wouldn't they?

To think otherwise was too painful to dwell on.

Bernice loved her adopted son. To her, Smokey was a gift who had filled her last seventeen years with joy.

And Bubba?

Ugly overbearing violent abusive Bubba.

He was a miserable fat drunken pig ... but when it came down to it, he was HER miserable fat drunken pig, and Bernice missed him terribly.

To keep dark thoughts at bay, she carried on as normal ... as if Bubba and Smokey were still there.

Every evening, Bernice placed three settings for dinner ... continued to fry Burger and Chips, Smokey's favourite, on Fridays before heading out with her best friend, Ermintrude, for their weekly date at the Bingo ... and every Saturday morning, no matter how hung-over, she would launder Smokey's and Bubba's unworn clothes.

****

It was 1:40pm and Bernice had just finished. She gathered the washing in her basket, stepped out into the backyard and started pegging the sheets, shirts and underpants onto the Whirligig.

As she worked, Bernice began to recall what had happened the previous night at Bingo.

... And she felt ashamed.

****

'Eye Petal ... I just need number ten and I've got a Full House!'

'Ruddy 'ell Bernie ... first prize is a Meat Tray! If you win can I come round yours for Steak?'

'That's a date petal ... you bring the Stout and Chocs and I'll rent a nice slushy movie!'

'Oooh ... make it that new 'un with Stevie Stiffbone! What's it called?'

'Knock Out Nooky'

'That's the one! Ooh it sounds dead good! Stevie plays a boxer who falls madly in love with a Princess but the King doesn't think he's good enough for his daughter ... that is until she gets abducted by Aliens and Stevie rescues her.'

'Oooh ... sounds dead romantic ... is it a true story?'

The Compere interrupted.

'Okay ladies and gents ... eyes down for a full house!'

'First up ... its lucky number seven'

Everybody looked down.

'Next ... we've got ...'

'Come on ... come on ... number 10 ... just say it!'

Bernice's eyes were fixed on the Compere ... staring daggers ... willing the words out of his mouth.

'Number TEN' willed Bernice

'Number ... TEN' announced the Compere

'BINGO!'

Bernice leapt from her seat, swung round and clawed her way to the aisle. As she barged her way through, her unfeasibly large knockers began to swing pendulously inside her flimsy blouse until the left one

... having gained far too much momentum ... liberated itself and promptly slapped into the face of an elderly gentlemen sitting next to Ermintrude.

'Get an eyeful did ya? ... Ya dirty Bugger!' guffawed the ecstatic Ermintrude ... who was on the verge of peeing herself with excitement.

And he certainly had! The old man couldn't help himself ... he hadn't seen such a whopper for nigh on forty years and in his excitement ... stretched out a hand and gave the wayward breast a crafty fondle as it passed.

Bernice paused just long enough to smile back at the man who was bouncing up and down in his seat, arms raised in triumph with his tongue hanging out.

'Now, now ... cheeky!' she purred before blowing him a kiss.

Bernice made her way to the stage, accepted the Meat Tray from the Compere ... who received a good old snogging for his trouble ... then returned triumphantly to her seat, pausing only for as long as it took to fondle the blissed out old man as she passed.

Later that evening ... as the crowd filed out through the foyer, Ermintrude and Bernice, who were rather the worse for drink, accosted the Pensioner.

'Eee love!' beckoned Ermintrude. 'Look at our lovely Meat Tray! Look at all that lovely meat!'

'Ooh yes!' agreed the Pensioner 'Looks like some nice cuts. And some drumsticks too! I'm partial to a bit of breast meeself!'

'Cheeky Bugger!' countered Ermintrude

'No sausage though' guffawed Bernice.

'Ooh, I think I can help in that department!'

Do you think so petal? Got enough to satisfy two ravenous young ladies!'

'Absolutely!'

There was a pause. Bernice and Ermintrude looked at each other.

Their eyes were bright with mischievous intent.

'Go on then love!'

And with that, they took hold of the old man, frogmarched him out into the street and down a dark alley. What then occurred was anyone's guess, suffice to say it was the best five minutes the old man had enjoyed since his youth, and what's more, when he emerged from the alley, stuffed inside the pockets of his overcoat were three chicken drumsticks, a lamb chop and two 'slapper-size' pairs of panties.

****

As she pegged the last of Bubba's pants to the line, Bernice resolved to forget the events of the previous night.

She picked up the laundry basket, turned and made her way back to the house.

Just then, she heard thunder.

'Typical!' she thought, held out a hand to feel for rain and turned back to the washing.

CHAPTER FORTY

When Smokey turned back to the Skipper, the old critter was gone.

Smokey looked over the side and there in the water, beside the outrigger, was a dolphin.

Seeing it there reminded Smokey of something ... a dream he had once had ... of a dolphin reassuring a lost surfer ... of knowledge received in the midst of a great ocean ... **beside a Sinking Island.**

Smokey and the Skipper smiled at each other. Both knew this to be a parting.

Now they had separate paths to follow.

Despite the briefness of their friendship - four months in all - theirs had been a fruitful relationship. For master and student it had brought much ...

... for Smokey, heaven

... for Kipper, the earth.

Smokey waved goodbye. Then he turned, picked up his paddle, steered the outrigger away from the tidal wave ... and began to stroke.

Smokey did not need to look back to gauge how the tidal wave was developing behind him. He knew what it felt like when the bottom dropped out of the ocean ahead of a wave ... could sense a horizontal trough giving way to a vertical wave face.

He was a surfer, after all.

Next second, Smokey felt himself lifted ... drawn towards the clouds.

Higher he went, the wind streaming through his hair as the compressed flow of air was driven upwards. With it was carried all manner of seabird including a Booby called Bobby who landed on top of Smokey's head.

Laughing, Smokey gently brushed the confused bird away. 'My wave!' he shouted, and watched as Bobby shot upwards and over the peaking crest to safety.

By the time Smokey himself reached the crest, Bobby's escape hatch had firmly shut. Not that Smokey cared, mind you. By now he was committed ... clawing the water with his paddle ... determined to gain forward momentum before reaching the curl.

Despite the wave's infinite length ... forming as it did a circle radiating outwards from Moonshine ... Smokey found he was positioned barely ten metres to the left of its highest peak. Glancing across his right shoulder, to Smokey's astonishment he saw what must have been a thousand donkeys gunning towards him. They were backdooring the peak ... bodysurfing donkeys ... charging in through the out door!

And at their head was Gary William.

For an instant, Smokey considered pulling back. After all, the donkeys had priority and it was clear from the look of concentration on their faces and the alert forward posture of their ears, they were not about to give way to a shoulder hopper!

He needn't have worried though because donkeys are not wavehogs.

Instead, Gary caught Smokey's eye and with the slightest nod of his head, signalled to Smokey that he should go.

The left was all Smokey's.

The donkeys would go right!

Once again, Smokey dropped his head and dug his paddle hard into the water. He had to get his outrigger down the wave face. Had to make his turn.

As the earth spawned ancestor of countless Watersplashes began to break, Smokey felt the outrigger become weightless. Her bow dropped and like a bullet, she fell from the sky into a driven free fall.

Smokey moved to plant his paddle into the wave face but changed his mind.

He remembered himself ...

... Remembered ...

HE WAS A SURFER.

'Stuff that!' he screamed, threw the paddle aside and sprung to his feet which planted firmly on the port side of the outrigger ... right in front of the left. Smokey crouched and stuck his left arm out. His fingers found the water and he tensed his hand. The rush was tremendous but Smokey held firm until the port side of the outrigger was stalled by the tiniest fraction required to trim her on the sixpence of her hull still connected to the wave face.

At once the whole length of the outrigger connected with the water some four hundred feet above the wave's trough ... and six hundred beneath its pitching curl. It was the perfect position. Amazingly, Smokey found himself trimming smoothly across the water. He was slotted ... the outrigger beneath his feet, tracking on a course all its own ... but one which satisfied her rider.

As the biggest wave ever to accommodate mortal man began to tube over him, Smokey cross-stepped to the bow, threw his arms above his head and hung his toes over the nose.

And there he stayed ... perched like an eagle ... all seeing witness to the light made bright by the darkness surrounding it. Smokey, encircled by the wave ... untouched ... sheltered within, staring out.

And as that wave ... that Watersplash bulldozed its course over the ocean ... over Morningtaria and every other land ... it roared the roar of a billion lions.

And above it all ... above the cacophony, was heard the excited hoot of a young surfer called Smokey Kingfish ...

'WOOHOO!'

THE END

Epilogue

'Flamin Hell!' the man cursed. A big man at that ... a big man with tanned leathery skin.

More tanned and leathery than it had once been.

A big man ... to be sure. But definitely not as big as he had once been.

Why?

Well, the tanned leathery big man was a complete buffoon when it came to catching fish ... and no fish meant no breakfast, no lunch and no dinner.

Hence the cursing ... and hence the shrinkage.

He had just lost another one.

A fish that is.

But not always.

Yesterday ... he had lost a hook. The day before that ... a rod ... over the side of his upturned hull.

After cursing, the tanned leathery big man started again. He cast his line and sat for another few hours ... hoping to get another bite.

After all, what else was there to do?

Nothing.

He was stuck in the middle of nothingness. A never-ending glassy nothingness stretching towards an empty horizon in every direction.

But what was that?

A speck in the distance.

A speck which grew bigger until eventually it turned into a small boat, an outrigger, which drifted up to and bumped into the tanned leathery big man's upturned hull.

'Alright Dad!' said its occupant.

'Hello Smokey' replied Bubba 'Got any fish?'

****